W9-AGM-365

VAQUITA AND OTHER STORIES

VAQUITA

AND OTHER STORIES

EDITH PEARLMAN

UNIVERSITY OF PITTSBURGH PRESS

Published by the University of Pittsburgh Press,

Pittsburgh, Pa. 15260

Copyright © 1996, University of Pittsburgh Press

Manufactured in the United States of America

Printed on acid-free paper

10 9 8 7 6 5 4 3 2 1

Library of Congress Cataloging-in-Publication Data

will be found at the end of this book.

A CIP catalog record for this book is available

from the British Library.

for

Chester Pearlman

and

Rose Moss

CONTENTS

VAQUITA AND OTHER STORIES

VAQUITA

"Some day," said the minister of health to her deputy assistant, "you must fly me to one of those resort towns on the edge of the lake. Set me up in a striped tent. Send in kids who need booster shots. The mayor and I will split a bottle of cold Spanish wine; then we will blow up the last storehouse of canned milk . . ."

The minister paused. Caroline, the deputy, was looking tired. "Lina, what godforsaken place am I visiting tomorrow?" the minister asked.

"Campo del Norte," came the answer. "Water adequate, sewage okay, no cholera, frequent dysentery . . ."

Señora Marta Perera de Lefkowitz, minister of health, listened and memorized. Her chin was slightly raised, her eyelids half-lowered over pale eyes. This was the pose that the newspapers caricatured most often. Pro-government papers did it more or less lovingly—in their cartoons the minister resembled an inquisitive cow. Opposition newspapers accentuated the lines under Señora Perera's eyes and adorned her mouth with a cigarette, and never omitted the famous spray of diamonds on her lapel.

"There has been some unrest," Caroline went on.

Señora Perera dragged on a cigarette—the fourth of her daily five. "What kind of unrest?"

"A family was exiled."

"For which foolishness?"

The deputy consulted her notes. "They gave information to an Australian writing an exposé of smuggling in Latin America."

"Horrifying. Soon someone will suggest that New York launders our money. Please continue."

"Otherwise, the usual. Undernourishment. Malnourishment. Crop failures. Overfecundity."

Señora Perera let her eyelids drop all the way. Lactation had controlled fertility for centuries, had kept population numbers steady. In a single generation the formula industry had changed everything; now there was a new baby in every wretched family every year. She opened her eyes. "Television?"

"No. A few radios. Seventy kilometers away there's a town with a movie house."

Golden dreams. "The infirmary—what does it need?"

Again a shuffling of papers. "Needles, gloves, dehydration kits, tetanus vaccine, cigarettes . . ."

A trumpet of gunfire interrupted the list.

The minister and her deputy exchanged a glance and stopped talking for a minute. The gunshots were not repeated.

"They will deport me soon," Señora Perera remarked.

"You could leave of your own accord," said Caroline softly.

"That idea stinks of cowshit," Señora Perera said, but she said it in Polish. Caroline waited. "I'm not finished meddling," added the Señora in an inaudible conflation of the languages. "They'll boot me to Miami," she continued in an ordinary tone, now using only Spanish. "The rest of the government is already there, except for Perez, who I think is dead. They'll want my flat, too. Will you rescue Gidalya?"

Gidalya was the minister's parrot. "And while you're at it, Lina, rescue this department. They'll ask you to run the health services, whichever putz they call minister. They'll appreciate that only you can do it—you with principles, but no politics. So do it."

"Take my bird, take my desk, take my job . . ." Caroline sighed.

"Then that's settled."

They went on to talk of departmental matters—the medical students' rebellion in the western city; the girl born with no hands who had been found in a squatters' camp, worshipped as a saint. Then they rose.

Caroline said, "Tomorrow morning Luis will call for you at five."

"Luis? Where is Diego?"

"Diego has defected."

"The scamp. But Luis, that garlic breath—spare me."

"An escort is customary," Caroline reminded her.

"This escort may bring handcuffs."

The two women kissed formally; all at once they embraced. Then they left the cool, almost empty ministry by different exits. Caroline ran down to the rear door; her little car was parked in back. Señora Perera took the grand staircase that curved into the tiled reception hall. Her footsteps echoed. The guard tugged at the massive oak door until it opened. He pushed back the iron gate. He bowed. "Good evening, Señora Ministra."

She waited at the bus stop—a small, elderly woman with dyed red hair. She wore one of the dark, straight-skirted suits that, whatever the year, passed for last season's fashion. The diamonds glinted on its lapel.

Her bus riding was considered an affectation. In fact it was an indulgence. In the back of an official limousine she felt like a corpse. But on the bus she became again a young medical student in Prague, her hair in a single red braid. Sixty years ago she had taken trams everywhere—to cafés; to the apartment of her lover; to her Czech tutor, who became a second lover. In her own room she kept a sweet songbird. At the opera she wept at Smetana. She wrote to her parents in Krakow whenever she needed money. All that was before the Nazis, before the war, before the partisans; before the year hiding out in a peasant's barn, her only company a cow; before liberation, DP camp, and the ship that sailed west to the New World.

Anyone who cared could learn her history. At least once a year somebody interviewed her on radio or television. But the citizens were interested mainly in her life with the cow. "Those months in the barn—what did you think about?" She was always asked that question. "Everything," she sometimes said. "Nothing," she said, sometimes. "Breast-feeding," she barked, unsmiling, during the failed campaign against the formula companies. They called her *La Vaca*—The Cow.

The bus today was late but not yet very late, considering that a revolution was again in progress. So many revolutions had erupted since she arrived in this plateau of a capitol, her mother gasping at her side. The Coffee War first, then the Colonels' Revolt, then the . . . Here was the bus, half full. She grasped its doorpost and, grunting, hauled herself aboard. The driver, his eyes on the diamonds, waved her on; no need to show her pass.

The air swam with heat. All the windows were closed against stray bullets. Señora Perera pushed her own window open. The other passengers made no protest. And so, on the ride home, the minister, leaning on her hand, was free to smell the diesel odor of the center of the city, the eucalyptus of the park, the fetidity of the river, the thick citrus stink of the remains of that day's open market, and finally the hibiscus scent of the low hills. No gunshots disturbed the journey. She closed the window before getting off the bus and nodded at the five people who were left.

In the apartment, Gidalya was sulking. New visitors always wondered at a pet so uncolorful—Gidalya was mostly brown. "I was attracted by his clever rabbinical stare," she'd explain. Gidalya had not mastered even the usual dirty words; he merely squawked, expressing a feeble rage. "Hola," Señora Perera said to him now. He gave her a resentful look. She opened his cage, but he remained on his perch, picking at his breast feathers.

She toasted two pieces of bread and sliced some papaya and poured a glass of wine and put everything on a tray. She took the tray out onto the patio and, eating and smoking, watched the curfewed city below. She could see a bit of the river, with its Second Empire bridge and ornamental stanchions. Half a mile north was the plaza, where the cathedral of white volcanic stone was whitened further by floodlamps; this pale light fizzed through the leafy surround. Bells rang faintly. Ten o'clock.

Señora Perera carried her empty tray back into the kitchen. She turned out the lights in the living room and flung a scarf over Gidalya's cage. "Goodnight, possibly for the last time," she said, first in Spanish and then in Polish. In her bedroom, she removed the diamonds from her lapel and fastened them onto the jacket she would wear in the morning. She got ready for bed, got into bed, and fell instantly asleep.

Some bits of this notable widow's biography were not granted to interviewers. She might reminisce about her early days here—the resumption of medical studies and the work for the new small party on the left—but she never mentioned the expensive abortion paid for by her rich, married lover. She spoke of the young Federico Perera, of their courtship, of his growing prominence in the legal profession, of her party's increasing strength and its association with various coalitions. She did not refer to Federico's infidelities, though she knew their enemies made coarse jokes about the jewelry he gave her whenever he took a new mistress. Except for the diamonds, all the stuff was fake.

In her fifties she had served as minister of culture; under her warm attention both the National Orchestra and the National Theater thrived. She was proud of that, she told interviewers. She was proud, too, of her friendship with the soprano Olivia Valdez, star of light opera, now retired and living in Tel Aviv; but she never spoke of Olivia. She spoke instead of her husband's merry North American nieces, who had often flown down from Texas. She did not divulge that the young Jewish hidalgos she presented to these girls found them uncultivated. She did not mention her own childlessness. She made few pronouncements about her adopted country; the famous quip that revolution was its national pastime continued to embarrass her. The year with the cow? I thought about everything. I thought about nothing.

What kind of cow was it?

Dark brown, infested with ticks, which I got, too.

Your name for her?

My Little Cow, in two or three tongues.

The family who protected you?

Righteous Gentiles.

Your parents?

In the camps. My father died. My mother survived. I brought her to this country.

. . . Whose air she could never breathe. Whose slippery words she refused to learn. I myself did not need to study the language; I remembered it from a few centuries earlier, before the expulsion from Spain. Nothing lightened Mama's mood; she wept every night until she died.

Señora Perera kept these last gloomy facts from interviewers. "The people here—they are like family," she occasionally said. "Stubborn as pigs," she once added, in a cracked mutter that no one should have heard, but the woman with the microphone swooped on the phrase as if it were an escaping kitten.

"You love this sewer," shouted Olivia during her raging departure.

"You have no children to love, and you have a husband not worth loving, and you don't love me anymore because my voice is cracking and my belly sags. So you love my land, which I at least have the sense to hate. You love the oily generals. The aristocrats scratching them-selves. The intellectuals snoring through concerts. The revolutionaries in undershirts. The parrots, even! You are besotted!"

It was a farewell worthy of Olivia's talents. Their subsequent corre-spondence had been affectionate. Olivia's apartment in Israel would become Señora Perera's final home; she'd fly straight to Tel Aviv from Miami. The diamonds would support a few years of simple living. But for a little while longer she wanted to remain amid the odors, the rap blaring from pickup trucks, the dance halls, the pink evangelical churches, the blue school uniforms, the highway's dust, the river's tarnish. To remain in this wayward place that was everything a barn was not.

Luis was waiting for her at dawn, standing beside the limousine. He wore a mottled jumpsuit.

"Much trouble last night?" she asked, peering in vain into his sunglasses while trying to avoid his corrupt breath.

"No," he belched, omitting her title, omitting even the honorific. This disrespect allowed her to get into the front of the car like a pal.

At the airport they climbed the steps of a tipsy little plane. Luis stashed his Uzi in the rear next to the medical supplies. He took the copilot's seat. Señora Perera and the nurse—a Dutch volunteer with passable Spanish—settled themselves on the other two buckets. Señora Perera hoped to watch the land fall away, but from behind the pilot's shoulder she could see only sky, clouds, one reeling glimpse of high-way, and then the mountainside. So she reconstructed the city from memory: its mosaic of dwellings enclosed in a ring of hills, its few tall structures rising in the center like an abscess. The river, the silly Parisian bridge. The plaza. People were gathering there now, she guessed, to hear today's orations.

The Dutch nurse was huge, a goddess. She had to hunch her shoulders and let her big hands dangle between her thighs. Some downy thatch sprouted on her jaw; what a person to spend eternity with if this light craft should go down, though there was no reason you should be stuck forever with the dullard you happened to die with. Señora Perera planned to loll on celestial pillows next to Olivia. Federico might join them every millennium or so, good old beast, and Gidalya, too, prince of rabbis released from his avian corpus, his squawks finally making sense . . . She offered her traveling flask to the nurse. "Dutch courage?" she said in English. The girl smiled without comprehension, but she did take a swig.

In less than an hour they had flown around the mountain and were landing on a cracked tar field. A helicopter stood waiting. Señora Perera and the nurse used the latrine. A roll of toilet paper hung on a nail, for their sakes.

And now they were rising in the chopper. They swung across the hide of the jungle. She looked down on trees flaming with orange flowers and trees foaming with mauve ones. A sudden clearing was immediately swallowed up again by squat, broad-leafed trees. Lime green parrots rose up together—Gidalya's rich cousins.

They landed in the middle of the town square beside a chewed bandstand. A muscular functionary shook their hands. This was Señor Rey, she recalled from Lina's instructions. Memory remained her friend; she could still recite the names of the cranial nerves. Decades ago, night after night, she had whispered them to the cow. She had explained the structures of various molecules. *Ma Petite Vache . . .* She had taught the cow the Four Questions.

Señor Rey led them toward a barracks mounted on a slab of cement: the infirmary she had come to inspect. The staff—a nurse-director and two assistants—stood stiffly outside as if awaiting arrest. It was probable that no member of any government had ever before visited—always excepting smugglers.

The director, rouged like a temptress, took them around the scrubbed infirmary, talking nonstop. She knew every detail of every case history; she could relate every failure from undermedication, from wrong medication, from absence of medication. The Dutch girl seemed to understand the rapid-fire Spanish.

Surgical gloves, recently washed, were drying on a line. The store-room shelves held bottles of injectable Ampicillin and jars of Valium—folk remedies now. A few people lay in the rehydration room. In a corner of the dispensary a dying old man curled upon himself. Behind a screen Señora Perera found a listless child with swollen glands and pale nail beds. She examined him. A year ago she would have asked the parents' permission to send him to a hospital in the city for tests and treatment if necessary. Now the hospital in the city was dealing with wounds and emergencies, not diseases. The parents would have refused anyway. What was a cancer unit for but to disappear people? She stood for a moment with her head bowed, her thumb on the child's groin. Then she told him to dress himself.

As she came out from behind the screen she could see the two nurses through a window. They were walking toward the community kitchen to inspect the miracle of *soya* cakes. Luis lounged just outside the window.

She leaned over the sill and addressed his waxy ear. "Escort those two, why don't you? I want to see Señor Rey's house alone."

Luis moved sullenly off. Señor Rey led her toward his dwelling in resentful silence. Did he think she really cared whether his cache was guns or cocaine? All she wanted was to ditch Luis for a while. But she would have to subject this village thug to a mild interrogation just to get an hour's freedom.

And then she saw a better ruse. She saw a motorbike, half concealed in Señor Rey's shed.

She had flown behind Federico on just such a bike, one summer by the sea. She remembered his thick torso within the circle of her arms. The next summer she had driven the thing herself, Olivia clasping her waist.

"May I try that?"

Señor Rey helplessly nodded. She handed him her kitbag. She hiked up her skirt and straddled the bike. The low heels of her shoes hooked over the footpieces.

But this was not flying. The machine strained uphill, held by one of the two ruts they called a road. On the hump between the ruts grass grew and even flowers—little red ones. She picked up speed slightly and left the village behind. She passed poor farms and thick growths of vegetation. The road rose and fell. From a rise she got a glimpse of a brown lake. Her buttocks smarted.

When she stopped at last and got off the bike, her skirt ripped with a snort. She leaned the disappointing machine against a scrub pine and she walked into the woods, headed toward the lake. Mist encircled some trees. Thick roots snagged her shoes. But ahead was a clearing, just past tendrils hanging from branches. A good place for a smoke. She parted the vines and entered, and saw a woman.

A girl, really. She was eighteen at most. She was sitting on a carpet of needles and leaning against a harsh tree. But her lowered face was as untroubled as if she had been resting on a silken pouf. The nursing infant was wrapped in coarse, striped cloth. Its little hand rested against her brown breast. Mother and child were outwardly motionless, yet Señora Perera felt a steady pulsing beneath her soles, as if the earth itself were a giant teat.

Señora Perera did not make much of a sound, only her old woman's wheeze. But the girl looked up as if in answer, presenting a bony, pockmarked face. If the blood of the conquistadors had run in her ancestor's veins, it had by now been conquered; she was utterly Indian. Her flat brown eyes were fearless.

"Don't get up, don't trouble yourself..." But the girl bent her right leg and raised herself to a standing position without disturbing the child.

She walked forward. When she was a few feet away from Señora Perera, her glance caught the diamonds. She looked at them with mild interest and returned her gaze to the stranger.

They faced each other across a low dry bush. With a clinician's calm Señora Perera saw herself through the Indian girl's eyes. Not a grandmother, for grandmothers did not have red hair. Not a soldier, for soldiers did not wear skirts. Not a smuggler, for smugglers had ingratiating manners. Not a priest, for priests wore combat fatigues and gave out cigarettes; and not a journalist, for journalists piously nodded. She could not be a deity; deities radiated light. She must then be a witch.

Witches have authority. "Good that you nurse the child," said Señora Perera.

"Yes. Until his teeth come."

"After his teeth come, *chica*. He can learn not to bite." She opened her mouth and stuck out her tongue and placed her forefinger on its tip. "See? Teach him to cover his teeth with his tongue."

The girl slowly nodded. Señora Perera mirrored her nod. Jew and Indian: Queen Isabella's favorite victims. Four centuries later, Jews were a great nation, getting richer. Indians were multiplying, getting poorer. It would be a moment's work to unfasten the pin and pass it across the bush. But how would the girl fence the diamonds? Señor Rey would insist on the lion's share; and what would a peasant do with money anyway—move to the raddled capitol? Señora Perera extended an empty hand toward the infant and caressed its oblivious head. The mother revealed a white smile.

"He will be a great man," promised the Señora.

The girl's sparse lashes lifted. Witch had become prophetess. The incident needed only a bit of holy nonsense for prophetess to become lady. "He will be a great man," Señora Perera repeated, in Polish, stalling for time. And then, in Spanish again, with the hoarseness that inevitably accompanied her quotable pronouncements, "Suckle!" she commanded. She unhooked the pin. With a flourishing gesture right out of one of Olivia's operettas, conveying tenderness and impetuousness and authority too, she pressed the diamonds into the girl's free hand. "Keep them until he's grown," she hissed, and she turned on her heel and strode along the path, hoping to disappear abruptly into the floating mist as if she had been assumed. *Penniless exile crawls into Tel Aviv,* she thought, furious with herself.

When she reached the motorbike, she lit the postponed cigarette and grew calm again. After all, she could always give Spanish lessons.

Señor Rey was waiting in front of his shed. He clucked at her ripped skirt. And Luis was waiting near the helicopter, talking to the pilot. The Dutch nurse would stay until next Saturday, when the mail Jeep would arrive. So it was just the three of them, Luis said with emphasis, giving the unadorned lapel a hard stare. She wondered if he would arrest her in the chopper, or upon their arrival at the airstrip, or in the little plane, or when they landed at the capitol, or not until they got to her apartment. It didn't matter; her busybody's career had been honorably completed with the imperative uttered in the clearing. Suckle. Let *that* word get around—it would sour all the milk in the country, every damned little jar of it.

And now—deportation? Call it retirement. She wondered if the goons had in mind some nastier punishment. That didn't matter, either; she'd been living on God's time since the cow.

CAVALIER

⌒⌒⌒⌒⌒⌒⌒⌒⌒⌒⌒⌒⌒⌒⌒⌒⌒

Gifford van Valkenburgh was as thin as a pike. On top of the pike his head waggled a little. His hair, a whitened yellow, sprang abundantly from his high forehead and sparsely from the sides of his neck. It sprouted in the mysterious recesses of his ears. Mustache and eyebrows were thick, too. The long torso was bent in the middle of the back. The shallow angle of this deformity measured one hundred and sixty degrees, by his estimate. "You see the identical crook in many of the figures in Daumier," he said to Lolly Perkins on the day of her interview.

"Does it hurt—your back?"

"No," he told her. "Skeletal problems tend to correct themselves during the fifties, though stiffness remains, and disfigurement. Do you want to know what comes afterwards?"

"If you want to tell me."

He noted the freshness of the skin on her buck-toothed face. "The sixties is given over to digestive disorders," he said. "A new one every week. By the time you're seventy your diet has been restricted to warm water and powdered fiber. Your organs just manage to convert incoming mush into outgoing. Then comes the decade of mortal diseases."

Now he flashed his eyes at her from under the birch-twig brows. This was a trick he'd developed during his early years when part of his job was to meet in tutorial with some even younger historian. The student's attention sometimes wandered away like a donkey. Gifford's sudden gleam would resettle the beast.

"Mortal diseases," Lolly prompted.

"Well, they mean to kill you. But if you happen to survive, you'll find the eighties uneventful, though somewhat isolated. I don't mind isolation." He glinted at her, again in a more or less friendly fashion. "I *prefer* solitude."

"Your son thinks you should have a live-in," said Lolly.

"To blow my nose? To teach me hop-hip?"

She giggled briefly. Then: "You might set yourself on fire, living here alone. You could break your leg and no one would know and you'd die of dehydration."

"And your presence will insure that I die of stroke instead. Or maybe pneumonia."

She nodded without speaking. Her soft lips almost met over her big teeth. "Those are nicer deaths."

He had nearly chosen her then. Instead he indicated that the interview was over. He sat through three more candidates. The first was an out-of-work physical therapist whose hair was dyed blond. The poor man tried to reign in his loose tongue, but he couldn't stop chattering. The second was a retired baby nurse, a *mulato*. Gifford was charmed by the sweet island voice; but he knew that her professionalism would age him further without doing him in. Finally came a young musician who had studied some Central American history and could quote from Prescott's *Conquest of Mexico*. "'The Spaniard, with his nice point of honor, high romance, and proud, vainglorious vaunt, was the true representative of the age of chivalry. Arms was the only profession worthy of gentle blood.'"

Gifford glanced with sympathy at this applicant. The boy had no doubt looked up Gifford's biography, maybe even glanced through the books; but he had decided that quoting the van Valkenburgh histories of Mexico would be too obvious a ploy. So he had memorized a bit out of an earlier historian. Clever, too clever perhaps . . . "Why do you want to play nanny to a frail old man?"

"I need a break from music. I need to practice—I'm glad you have a piano—but I'm not ready to return to performance." Gifford waited. "I'm a good nurse. I buried my partner not long ago." And indeed his eyes looked as if they were still smarting.

That Friday, on the weekly visit to his son and daughter-in-law, Gifford announced his choice. "I'll take that girl. What's her name again—Silly?"

"Lolly."

"Lolly. She's inexperienced and ignorant and overweight. She'll serve me right for living too long."

"She's not . . ." his son Monte began, and then decided against comment. Monte knew Lolly from his own interviews—he had screened twelve candidates. During her one year at a state university, before leaving the prairie for New England, she had volunteered on the surgical unit of the local hospital. She liked to read. She liked math problems.

"That hairdo," sighed the old man. "That slobbish clothing." Lolly's curly reddish hair had been scraped into two bunches behind her ears. For the interview she had worn a jeans skirt and a striped overblouse.

Fay van Valkenburgh assured her father-in-law that everyone on Lolly's list of references had praised her meticulousness. "And you've got your housekeeper for everyday cleaning and meals. Lolly won't be slobbish where you are concerned—medications and so forth."

"I can count my own damned pills."

Fay did not remind him that though he could count his pills he sometimes failed to distinguish among them. The recent accidental overdose of Coumadin had scared them all.

"I prefer women to be pretty," Gifford said, but it was a thrust of admiration, not hostility. Fay fingered her chignon—a leftover style that suited her; and when her hair was loose on the pillow Monte still liked to bury his nose in its bronze and gray ripples. Two rip-snorting old parties of sixty, she thought with satisfaction, and then she felt the eyes of her father-in-law fasten on her neck like the mandibles of some selfish insect. This girl Lolly seemed competent, Fay thought; let's just hope he doesn't offend her, he's getting irritable and sometimes confused. It was sad . . . She touched her hair again, this time at the brow; better keep those neurons in place.

Lolly moved in on a Wednesday in May. A friend she'd made during her two months of temporary office work drove her over from the Somerville rooming house. Girl and boy carried in a quilt, a portable stereo, tapes, a pillow, and two suitcases. Gifford watched from his chair in the living room. She owned only one small crate of paperbacks; perhaps she was planning to ransack his library. Finally they lugged between them a large stainless steel box—a safe, Gifford thought. "My microwave," Lolly explained, and led the way into the pantry. Gifford heard a faint clunk. They had put the thing on the side counter next to the copper ice bucket that hadn't been used in thirty years, under the shelves that held his dead wife's collection of cups. Why did Silly need a microwave? Wasn't the old oven fast enough to heat the dinners the housekeeper left for him?

"I'll be off, then, Loll," said the boy, walking backward through the hall as if expecting a tip. "Good-bye, Professor Vandenberg."

". . . van Valkenburgh," Lolly was saying in the vestibule. "Ricky, thanks a million."

And then she was standing in the living room. Her hair was dark orange and her face was pink and her shirt was yellow. She was like an overexposure: a dull glow in the sepia sadness of this Cambridge room. He thought of Cortes approaching Montezuma, Cortes so ruddy, Montezuma gray with fear. The Spaniard thought the Aztec was an emperor, or at least a king; but Montezuma was only a chief among chiefs, elected, deposable . . . Lolly strolled around the living room, her hands behind her back. She examined the Dutch painting over the fireplace —shaggy cows under a drooping tree. He had inherited that; but he had bought the pair of masks next to it back in the days when only a few collectors were interested in pre-Columbian stuff. She looked at the pencil drawing of Prescott's profile. "William Prescott," she read. "The famous historian," she identified. She looked at the fringed lamp and at the studio portrait of Gifford's sons as boys, little Monte, littler Hernando. "Sailor collars, cute," Lolly murmured. She paused in front of the glass-fronted case that contained a spear and a fragment from a journal in Spanish. She moved to the upright piano and touched middle C. She fingered the leather decanter that stood on a little round table. Should he offer her sherry? At last she sat down in the chair opposite his.

"Me cuenta su vida," she said.

"Cuent*e*," he corrected. Then he narrowed his eyes rather than widening them; this was the look that had alarmed doctoral examinees just before he shook their hands and told them they had passed with honors. "The story of my life? Where shall I begin? And how much time do you have? But no, Ms. Perkins, not to worry. I hate talking about myself."

The neighbors were delighted to welcome her. The professor next door confessed to Monte that he had found the sight of the bent old man and his cane dismayingly allegorical—Feeble Determination, maybe. Now Health marched beside him, a friendly personification who quickly learned the names of everybody on the block of narrow porched houses, and then the names of their children and nannies and dogs, and even the names of some of their cats. She knew who was away on vacation and who had come home. She even kept a concerned eye on the fungus spreading on the lawn across the street.

Gifford's housekeeper was satisfied. "Cleans up after herself."

"She's convenient at crossings," Gifford himself said to Monte. "She doesn't blather."

The routine of his days didn't change. He and Lolly shared an early breakfast of cold cereal and tea. Gifford wore a dressing gown over his pajamas. Lolly wore her usual denim and cotton rags. They read the several newspapers. During the meal the housekeeper banged open the back door. Neither of them winced.

After breakfast he retired to his room for an hour. "You are not to manage my bowels or my baths," he warned her the first morning.

"I'm only supposed to manage pills," she said evenly.

When he came downstairs, his thick hair gleamed. He was dressed in a jacket resembling the blazers of his youth and a pair of chinos like those his sons had worn. She quickly shoved her paperback into her jeans pocket. They walked together toward the university library, stopping when Gifford couldn't avoid greeting someone, or when he wanted to make an instructional comment. A family of finches were nesting under an eave—a rare bird to find in an urban setting. The variety store had changed hands again—Koreans had taken over from the Indians who had earlier bought out the Italians.

"Immigration patterns writ small," he said.

"Watch the curb, Mr. Van."

He put a hand on her shoulder while climbing the shallow stone steps of the library. Inside, on the grand marble staircase, he held onto the brass rail. Three further stairs led to the stacks. Once there, they used the tiny elevator. He sat at his carrel, and she sat nearby, reading her paperback. Whenever he wanted a book she fetched it for him. She became adept at computer searches, and she soon knew the layout of the place without having to consult the wall map; but she wasn't instantaneous, and he always started a headache while waiting for her return. He looked out of the window, so narrow that he felt like shooting from it. The summer students wandered listlessly to their classes in journal writing, cinema, the Vietnam War. These days not many young people were interested in the history of the conquest. Those who were interested signed up for Latin American studies; they learned that indigenous people were martyrs and that Spaniards were spoiled boys. Revisionism; it had been going on since Thucydides. Well, Gifford had been a bit of a revisionist too—one of the first to refuse to call human sacrifice barbarian. His earliest paper, sixty years ago, had compared the ceremonial cannibalism of the Aztecs to communion . . . Here she was, the book he wanted in her rosy hand.

They walked home. His fatigue always surprised him; then he remembered that he'd been flagging at this time of day for years. Lunch was leftovers popped into the microwave, an agreeable servant. Then came the lizard oblivion of the siesta. He awoke in a bad humor, but sherry restored him. News, and dinner, and a game of chess; Lolly was a mediocre opponent. He was soon ready again for sleep. She gave him his pills in the living room. He left her there, with her paperback.

"I've never heard of those writers she reads," he said to Monte and Fay on a Friday night in July. "Their first names are always Margaret or some Margaret diminutive."

"Drabble, Atwood, Piercy," Fay guessed. "Noonan? Anyway, she's not illiterate."

"Does she lock the windows every night?" said Monte, ever the worrier.

"Yes," said Gifford, watching Fay carry the plates into the kitchen. He had no idea whether Lolly locked up. He had no idea what she did after she gave him his nine o'clock pills. *He* undressed and went immediately to sleep—the tranquilizer did that for him, night after night after night, even though Hernando, psychiatrist to the stars out in Beverly Hills, had warned him ten years ago against developing a tolerance. "No tolerance yet," he snorted now.

"What did you say, Dad?" said Monte.

"Nothing. Thinking." He hated these slippings of the gears: talking to the absent, ignoring the present; alert to the dead, blind to the quick. He got up and unhooked his cane from the spindle of his Shaker chair and walked over to the enormous window that looked out onto the woods. It was eight-thirty, just growing dark. Raccoons and opossums lived among the flora of Lincoln, Massachusetts. Deer, too. The Aztecs had thought that the horses of the Spaniards were deer without antlers. They had thought too that deer and rider were one, a centaur with a breast of metal. That fantasy turned out to be prophetic; he knew Mexicans who were welded to their automobiles.

His eyes sought deer between the trees, found none, relaxed; and now he could no longer see even the trees, just the reflection of the white living room of this exurban sanctuary, and the flagstone fireplace, and his own son, sitting alone at the dining table.

Where *was* Lolly on Fridays? He napped after lunch, as usual. She was always gone when he awoke; he found his before-dinner pills in one dish and his bedtime ones in another, each dish labeled. The hours between four and six were long. By the time Monte came for him, his postsiesta irritability had developed into a full-fledged grudge—against the neighbor's dog, or the blameless housekeeper, or Hernando the ungrateful son—so that during the evenings at Monte's house he became easily snappish. Today he was raging at an article by some feminist, an article on La Malinche, Cortes's mistress. She was a chief's daughter, a member of a tribe perpetually at war with the Aztecs. She learned Spanish quickly; she soon became the captain's interpreter.

The writer of the article claimed that by these actions La Malinche betrayed her own people. Which people—the Aztecs who had disemboweled her father?

Monte was so patient, sitting there. "Was I lost in documents, when you were a boy?" Gifford asked without turning from the window.

"No."

"What kind of father was I?" he insisted.

Monte waited with a lawyerly caution. "You expected the best from us," he said at last.

"Demanding, then?"

"Not by my lights. You were always reasonable and soft spoken. So was Mom. Perhaps that's why I took up the trombone." He laughed, but his father didn't join him. "And maybe Hernando became a psychiatrist because you seemed sort of hidden."

"Hidden?"

"Well . . . You wanted something you weren't getting, though you didn't seem to want it from us, so we weren't unhappy, just, oh, curious . . ."

"Ah," the old man said, leaning a little too heavily on his cane and splaying a palm onto Fay's spotless window. Monte was beside him in an instant. "Wanted something?" Gifford said. "Doesn't everybody? No, I'm all right, thank you. Thank you."

It was around this time that a change began in him. His words sometimes ran together. His responses lagged. Fay called it a softening. To Monte it was a crumbling, as if that unsatisfied desire, whatever it was, was drying up, couldn't glue him together.

"What does Lolly think?" Fay asked her husband.

"Lolly thinks he's failing."

"Astute of her."

"There have been incidents, she says, tactfully."

Incidents was Gifford's word. Wet trousers, now and again; and stinking ones, too, one evening, after too much bean soup. She helped him strip and bathe that night. "You're not a practical nurse," he remarked from the tub, oddly unashamed, watching her swirl his underpants in the toilet. His thighs were as white and thin as young asparagus.

"I am a practical nurse, actually," was her cheerful reply. "By experience anyway." She wrung out the underpants and hung them on a towel rack and washed her hands and opened the bathroom door.

"Hey!"

"You don't need me now. Use the safety bar. Yell when you're in bed, and I'll bring you the nighttime pills."

"And a glass of sherry."

But she omitted the sherry. He was asleep before he had a chance to resent it.

The episodes of incontinence weren't repeated; but he developed a more alarming infirmity: insomnia. He had finally become tolerant to his pills. Doubling the dose didn't help.

He lay on his back, raking his hair with his hands. "Forget about sleeping," she said from the bedside chair he'd summoned her to. "It's relaxing that counts. Tell me your life."

He turned onto his side, his spine toward the window, his face toward her. His eyes were tightly shut. "No no no no."

"Somebody else's life, then."

"Separate the curtains?"

She got up and walked around the bed and did as he asked. He opened his eyes. A narrow band of light came from the streetlamp. It sliced across his hip; and then, as she resumed her seat and settled her gauzy skirt, it fell on her face.

He began with the life of Bernal Diaz, the campaigner who had written the only contemporary history of the conquest. Gifford fell asleep even before the first assault on the enemy. On the next night he continued with Diaz and finished him, or perhaps didn't. On subsequent nights he reminisced about other conquistadors—the treacherous Narvaez, the dark Olid, the faithful Alvarado. "Alvarado was my mother's family name," he said.

"Was your mother Spanish?" Her face was milky, like the moon.

"She was Mexican. Mestiza. Mostly Indian, I suspect. When she was angry she seemed an Aztec from the old days, ready to cut out your heart and eat it. I think that some ancestor of hers simply appropriated the Alvarado name." His speech and his intellect were restored at these times; the more he wandered during the day, the more collected he became at night.

"Go on."

"She would confront my father, raising her chin, raising her bosom. A warrior, I tell you. She tensed her buttocks. He was no match for her, poor old Dutchman. Though he was a distinguished clergyman, a clergyman-administrator, really, important posts all over the . . . world." His voice was thickening.

"You grew up in Mexico?"

But he had begun to snore.

He spent a week on Cortes. He reviewed the dissolute early years in Spain that gave no hint of the greatness to come. He told her of the assignment to Cuba, whose governor commissioned him to adventure against the mainland, and then repented of the commission and was about to remand it; Captain Cortes and his eager fleet departed in the dead of night. In Veracruz the captain made his lucky alliance with the Indian girl who would explain his words to the people of the land. "La Malinche was her name. The Spaniards renamed her Dona Marina. But the Indians called *him* Malintzin."

"In honor of her," suggested the soft voice.

"Not exactly in honor," he said, thinking of the feminist's article. "In acknowledgment."

The battles began immediately, he went on. The little army was never at rest. Sometimes women entered the fray. "Indian women, Spanish camp followers. Not only binding up their heroes—they fought, too, wearing rusty armor. The Aztec women could unhorse a soldier and then crush his stunned head with a rock . . . Does this distress you?"

"No."

"But of course the incisive battles, decisive I mean, were conducted by men, at the command of men, and they were as fierce and bloody as Waterloo and Verdun, but so personal, Lolly, only in the beginning did you get ranks against ranks, it was hand to hand very soon, hot and bloody and rancid. And Cortes in the thick of each fight. Captured only once, and about to be dragged off, but saved by a brave Indian ally, whose name he never learned . . . I tried to find it. I wasted a year on the research." He sighed, and slept.

He told her of Cortes's last decade, in Spain, unhonored and finally dishonored. Gifford was looking forward to the tragic finale of the death, no one there, the mistress gone, the wife gone, the children scattered, only a servant in attendance. But that episode happened to fall on a Friday, Lolly's half day off. Somehow during dinner at Monte's he forgot that she wouldn't be at his bedside later. He was good-humored throughout the evening, but he insisted on being taken home early. He entered the empty house, his son at his heels, and her absence hit him like a rain of arrows.

"Dad, Dad!" said Monte, trying to contain the shaking old man. Gifford freed himself and staggered to the plate of pills and swallowed them with a tumblerful of sherry rather than with the water she'd left him. He marched upstairs—slowly, but with a semblance of strength.

Monte followed at so discreet a distance that by the time he reached his father's room Gifford was asleep, fully clothed, on his bed. It was easy to undress him and to reclothe him in his pajamas, though Monte felt like a mortician.

He came downstairs to find Lolly in the hall. "Is something wrong?" she asked. "The movie got out late, and Ricky wanted—"

"I think everything is all right," said Monte, but really he did not know what to think. "He was enraged not to find you home," he said, wandering into the living room. "Childish of him," he hurried to add, though Lolly looked unbothered.

"He's been telling me history to fall asleep—to fall asleep himself, I mean. I stay awake because I find it so interesting. I even got *Captain from Castille* out of the library; a historical novel about the same period."

"I know." He remembered his father's contempt for that bestseller.

"He should have been one of them," Lolly said.

"I beg your pardon?"

"He should have gone for a soldier."

A *what?* "Sons of ministers don't become soldiers," he said.

She stood before him, silent as a captive.

Be sure to lock up . . . but he managed not to say that.

Gifford dispatched Cortes on Saturday and then began the life of Montezuma. "No one has ever written a psychobiography," he said. "Thank God. But he was certainly neurasthenic." There were long pauses now between sentences, and dry swallowings. Frequently she gave him water. He dribbled and dried his mouth with the back of his hand; his stomach was unsettled and noisy. But he produced a bit of the story every night. Montezuma was generous, and genteel, and fair. He was convinced that Cortes was his destiny. He refused to renounce the religion of his ancestors. "He allowed himself to be taken into the

Spanish camp, held hostage we would say today, to save the nation." Silence for several minutes: a false sleep. "He couldn't save it." An exhausted fart, and real sleep.

The next night a rock was thrown at Montezuma by one of his countrymen. He refused treatment and died of the wound. His people would not give him the burial due to chiefs. "Burial rites were as important to the Aztecs as to the Greeks. And so he was disgraced, even after death."

Gifford's favorite battle of the long contest was the Melancholy Night, when the Aztecs repelled the Spanish—favorite not because of the outcome, for he was neutral as to that, but because of the heroism on both sides. He described an ambush, the horses rearing, the men sliding from their backs; a collapse of causeways, earth tumbling into water; Indians in canoes hurling spears tipped with obsidian, and Spaniards leaping across canals; soldiers fighting soldiers on ground that shifted because it was not earth, not stones, but heaps of dying men. He was stirred but not overwrought; she did not attempt to still him. La Noche Triste replayed itself until long past midnight, the old man rumbling in his bed, the girl listening on her chair.

Early the next morning a stroke destroyed him. He lingered half a day in the hospital, speechless but not raging, able to communicate with Lolly, though all he wanted to convey, she told Monte in the visitors' sunroom, was his satisfaction with his sons and his work.

"Yet he would have preferred to lead men into war?" Monte said.

She met his sad gaze. "Or to follow," she said. "Yes, he would have preferred that."

At the graveside funeral Monte was impressed by her placidity, her calm refusal to ratchet up her emotions. She was less plain, he noticed, with her rusty hair worn loose, if loose were the word for such dense material. Her outfit—a black skirt and a U-necked blouse—revealed the positive influence of living near Harvard Square. But basically she was unchanged. It was his father who was changed—embalmed and encased in a coffin, but also linked, as if alive, to the girl who had last heard his voice. In the years to come, when Monte thought of his deep, dark-blooded parent, he would have to think also of Lolly.

"Who's the redhead?" whispered Hernando, who had blown in from the coast only yesterday.

"The live-in," said Monte. "I wrote you . . ."

"Ah, yes," said Hernando, still looking at her. "La Malinche, in a manner of speaking."

Your goddamn manner . . . The brothers bowed their heads as the coffin was lowered.

DONNA'S HEART

"I don't mind sleeping on the floor," Raphael said to Donna on one of their rare nights in her apartment. "It's getting up that's hard."

"Don't get up."

He didn't, not then. Later that morning, having in fact risen with agility, he busied himself with breakfast. He laughed at the muddle in her kitchen cabinets but offered no suggestions. This pleased Donna. Earlier that same week her cousin Josie, hands on hips in the living room, had started with a critique of the apartment and ended with a lengthy interpretation of Donna, her parents, her siblings, her education, and her pathology.

"For twenty years you've been preparing for this semidegradation," Josie declaimed. "Ever since you were fifteen. Boarding school gave you a conviction of your own worth and a need to work off your privilege. It made you feel noble and base at the same time. It gave you pride and it gave you . . ."

"I hated boarding school," said Donna from the couch. "I missed my mother."

Josie sighed and sat down. "She *was* lovely," she admitted. "Even tanked, she was lovely." Josie then turned brisk again. "And now you are exhibiting the same ambivalence toward the riches of life that the rich life has taught you. You work sixty hours a week in a soup kitchen and practice on an invaluable instrument. You're—"

"The harpsichord is insured."

"... you're on first names with some of the first families of the nation, but you spend your time with lowlife."

"Stop that."

"All right: with the wretched and impoverished. It's too bad your father pissed away that fortune; if you still had money you could work those sixty hours free instead of for peanuts. You have bones that a model would give her teeth for, and you dress like a lumberjack . . . Although I must admit that the other night, when Stuyvesant and I spotted you in that black dress, dining with that suitor of yours, you looked like royalty. At least from the distance."

Josie herself, with her red crest and her high little nose and her green walleyes, looked like a parrot. Raphael also was somewhat overcolored, Donna thought. His complexion was rubicund. His hair—receding, but dense in back and around the ears—was a pale yellow. No gray at all, though he had just turned fifty. His eyebrows were a similar gold. His eyes were deep blue. His suits were dark and perfectly cut, but his ties were explosions of color, almost illuminations. "He seems medieval," Josie was remarking. "Like a court physician. Jewish, you say?"

"I didn't say."

"A Jewish doctor," said Josie. "I know the type, Donna. The perfect companion for you. Self-indulgent where you are self-denying. Festive, to cut through your thundering seriousness. Able to enjoy money. Able to enjoy life!"

Donna bent over and elaborately retied her sneaker. "He's restrained in some ways," she found herself mumbling.

"Oh?"

"Conversationally," said Donna, looking up.

"Your father, my uncle, was never stingy with words."

"Rafe isn't stingy with anything. But he's careful of what he says."

Josie cocked her head. "And what does he say about this . . . domicile? No curtains, no rugs. Clothes in crates. Mattress on the floor."

"He has said nothing against it, and I've known him for a year."

"But I'll bet he sleeps at home."

Raphael did sleep at home. He still occupied the big house on Godolphin Hill where he'd lived for years, where he'd brought up three children, seen patients, cooked, and played Saturday night poker. From that house Rafe—and the kids, too, as soon as they were old enough—made frequent visits to the facility where his wife had resided since the youngest was three.

Now the children were grown. Raphael had regretfully procured a divorce, at poor Judith's insistence. His medical work was limited to occasional consultations; his eminence as a historian of mental illness—he was on the road a lot—precluded an ordinary psychiatric practice. But he saw no reason to give up his house. Grandchildren would visit some day. If he and Donna ever decided to live together, she could claim a room for herself. And another for her harpsichord.

Besides, he loved the place. He loved the nighttime view of city lights from the third-floor dormers. He loved the baronial hearth, the window seats, and the elegant kitchen which Judith had designed and assembled before her darkness descended for good. When Donna first entered that kitchen, she instantly commandeered the food processor. "Sooner or later somebody will donate one," she explained. "Then we'll return this to you."

Raphael smiled and helped her look for the feeder, which had rolled into one of the drawers. He rarely used the food processor—it was one of three his daughter had received as a wedding present. He never used the bread oven. Upstairs, though, he did use the electric towel warmer. That was another legacy from his long-ago wife, who had loved to offer herself to him immediately after a bath. *Post lavabum coitus,* they called the event—but how wet the bed would become. They needed hot towels to throw across the sheets; but by the time Rafe found a towel warmer in the Hammacher Schlemmer catalog, and ordered it, and received it, and plugged it in, Judith was gone. Rafe developed a taste for hot towels anyway.

He liked his oversized marital bed, too. Donna shared it with him on weekend nights and occasionally on weeknights if another staff member had the job of opening the Ladle the next morning—the job of hauling in bags of not-quite-stale bread left by the bakeries, putting cloths on the long tables, and welcoming the pale, red-nosed women who came by trolley from the Boston shelters, or who, convinced that danger lurked on those mostly empty trolleys, instead walked a mile, or two, or five.

Mostly, though, Donna spent weeknights in her own bed, Raphael in his.

And so, on Valentine's Day—a Tuesday, this year—they woke up in separate places, though at about the same time. Raphael had a plane to catch. He was giving two lectures in Chicago: one to the Classics Department at the university and the other to the Psychoanalytic Institute. The first was on *Heracles* and its healing message of not making grief your master. The professors would feel proud of Euripides. The second was called the Decoyed Soul—schizophrenia as seen by Ezekiel. The analysts would empathize with the prophet.

He awoke to his usual sweet sadness. Judith's tragedy, being alone, growing old. Then came the pleasanter thoughts of his children, and of Donna.

He had bought Donna a Valentine's gift. It was a piece of gold in the shape of a heart, or of a heart's periphery—there was nothing in its center. It was set with small rubies. It had rested on a cushion of velvet in a jeweler's window. He distrusted bought presents; he preferred the spontaneous giving away of one's own possessions. But he went in anyway. Was it brooch or pendant? he had asked the jeweler. Ah, that was a good question, the jeweler responded like a pedagogue; it was neither brooch nor pendant yet, exactly as an infant was neither male nor female in utero (how long had this throwback been slumbering?). The designer of the heart had guaranteed to attach either a fastening device or a loop and chain, whichever the customer desired. A pin of course would be a versatile addition to a wardrobe (Donna could wear it on that drippy black dress, Raphael supposed); a pendant admitted various lengths of chain, so that the heart could dwell in the hollow of the neck (that bony place!) or the bosom (she'd probably prefer that; she'd cover the thing with one of those plaid shirts and nobody would ever know it existed).

Could it be made into a ring? Raphael inquired.

The jeweler pressed the heart against Raphael's pinky—pale, freckled, blonde-threaded. The rubies looked like a bad joke. "I don't see why not."

So a ring it became. Now it lay on his dresser in a little gray box. He showered, used a hot towel, called a taxi, dressed, finished packing; and not until he was allowing the polite young cab driver to relieve him of his suitcase did he remember the box. He raced upstairs and discovered his plane ticket lying on the dresser too.

Donna operated the Ladle out of Godolphin Unitarian. Rafe asked the taxi to crawl down the alley behind the church and to wait in the rector's parking space. It was eight o'clock. The guests were beginning to arrive. Two of them were descending the short flight of stone steps into the basement. He followed them.

In the plain, yellow-walled dining room two volunteers were setting up long folding tables. Another was winding red crepe paper around the slender supporting poles. In the kitchen others were working at the counters and at the ancient black stove. Beth, Donna's second in command, told him that Donna was in storage—a chilling locution, but he knew what she meant. Donna was in a cold back room pulling potatoes from sacks. Some she was throwing into a rubbish bin, others into a low-wheeled cart, where lay also a plastic sack of ground meat. She looked up. Her large, colorless eyes widened further. He became acutely conscious of his cashmere coat. Regret seized him in the glands, like mumps. The ring could stay in his pocket. He'd been a fool to think she'd want such a thing. "Happy Valentine's Day," he said.

"Happy Valentine's Day." She stood composedly beside her dubious ingredients.

". . . a present," he said, and handed her the box.

She wiped her hands on her apron. She took the box and opened it. "Rafe!"

He bent over it with her as if he too were seeing it for the first time.

"Try it on," he said. The potatoes smelled terrible, or maybe the meat. "Shall I help you?"

But the ring was already wobbling on her fourth finger. "A little large," she said softly.

"It *should* be perfect."

"I have narrow fingers."

"But I swiped that other ring of yours, the one in the kitchen drawer. I got it measured and had this made the same size."

"My mother's rock? Oh, that's too big, too."

"I've seen it on your finger!"

"I use adhesive tape."

The exchange was beginning to resemble a fight. It seemed to be leading him somewhere—to a proposal of marriage, maybe, or to an irrevocable breakup. He would never know which, for they were interrupted by Nellie.

Nellie was one of the filthiest women Raphael had ever seen. During his internship in New York he had had to examine some disgusting patients; she reminded him of them. Her face was streaked with dirt and her nails were black. She was about thirty; he didn't like to think about how those thirty years had been lived. At least she was unaggressive, not one of the snarling vagrants that the untrained Donna dealt with so well. Nellie made little trouble. She ate alone, in a corner, scowling and sad. When it was time to leave (the Ladle served only breakfast and lunch), she would slouch around the room once or twice and then go away. She slept in doorways or on grates, Donna said. Twice she had been discovered sleeping in the windowless room where extra folding chairs were stored. This had troubled the directors of the church. Now Donna was careful to check the chair room before leaving.

Nellie said, "Aspirin."

"I'll be with you in about five minutes, Nellie," said Donna.

"Now," said Nellie.

"Wait for me by the medicine chest," said Donna.

"Fuck that," said Nellie.

Donna repeated "wait for me" in her unemphatic, uncontrolling way: Athena speaking to the Furies. Nellie vanished.

It was time for Rafe to vanish, too.

"I like the ring," said Donna.

"Perhaps you'll grow into it. I'll be back on Thursday."

He embraced her, more or less. They were standing on opposite sides of the cart, whose gamey contents offended their nostrils—his, anyway. The cart, shifting on its wheels, banged his shin.

At the door of storage, he looked back. She was sorting potatoes again. He passed Nellie standing by the medicine chest in the little office. In the big kitchen a volunteer was swearing at the food processor. Rafe showed her how to lock the pieces together. Outside, the cab was waiting, its motor still running.

On the drive to the airport he wondered how the ring would fare. Its looseness was a problem. Might it slide unnoticed into the rubbish bin? Or later, when Donna was plunging the toilet (the toilet overflowed at least once a day, she'd told him), might it slip off her finger and vanish into a swirl of excrement and tampons and (Donna sometimes thought) fetal tissue? More probably she would put it in a safe place for the day, tighten it with adhesive tape tomorrow, wear it Saturday night, and then drop it into the kitchen drawer. There it would keep company with bottle tops, an ivory teether, and her mother's five-carat diamond.

Donna did put the ring in a safe place—the deep front key pocket of her jeans, where it nestled against her groin. Every so often that morning she reached her hand under her apron and touched the little bulge. She touched it while interposing herself between two warring women, as if it would make them drop their weapons. The women did calm down—Beth drew the one with the knife into conversation, and Donna persuaded the other to put down the steaming coffee pot. Donna touched the bulge while listening to the incomprehensible babble of the Lithuanian woman. Perhaps contact with the ring would confer the gift of tongues. She touched it during her conversation with sweet Letitia, who was managing to hold onto the apartment the city had given her, and with Jocelyn, who wasn't drinking at all anymore, though her son was drinking more, and him only eighteen; and wasn't things going to get worse when them niggers moved into the project? "Jocelyn," warned Donna, her thumb caressing rubies under denim. Jocelyn said, "Shit, Donna, you know what I mean."

Generally she did know what they meant. She knew that whiskey warmed; that blows could seem to warm, too; that the face of the other, any other, could become monstrous in a minute. That a municipal office that appeared to be a calm arrangement of rectangles could become a funnel, could suck you in. She knew that a deformed plastic ashtray could be a precious relic (again she touched her valentine). She knew that the women she served trusted her, more or less—that is, they trusted her not to banish them casually, not to pink-slip them except in extreme situations, not to offer help beyond food and the use of the bathroom and a willing ear.

She had opened the Ladle six years ago. But ever since college she had found jobs in shelters and halfway houses and soup kitchens. So she had been at this work, whatever it was, for fourteen years. Whatever it was . . . "Saintly tasks," said her would-be acolytes—students from social work school or theological seminaries, young women who usually dropped away after a while, offended by the amount of bookkeeping an operation like this entailed, or turned off by the daily cleaning tasks, or repelled by the clientele. "Saintly tasks my backside," said Josie. "You're thumbing your nose at the aristocracy like your old man before you." Josie volunteered faithfully once a week, and the guests seemed to appreciate her outspokenness. Donna's mother, dead now for a decade, had responded to her daughter's choice of career with reminiscences about her own stretch at the *Catholic Worker*. "But I gave up slumming when I took up drink," she recalled in her hoarse and charming voice. "And I traded the church for your father. Fair exchanges, I thought. Still do. Not that *you* have to give up anything for anybody, darling, ever."

A local left-wing newspaper had described the Ladle variously as a Band-Aid, worse than nothing, enfeebling, disempowering. "I am manager of a soup kitchen for poor and homeless women," Donna had written beside "occupation" in her college's tenth reunion book. It didn't sound very different from owner of a flying school or proprietor of a bookshop, though it didn't much resemble patent attorney, oncologist, film editor, or diving instructor; and it seemed enormously different from member of the United States House of Representatives and talk show hostess. Donna was awed by these last two classmates; she couldn't imagine spending her own working hours speaking before an audience. Once or twice a month she had to present the Ladle's slide show to a church group or a reform club, and she needed to prime herself for the ordeal with two shots—that is, she *had* needed to liquor up until Raphael introduced her to the benzodiazepines. "No, one milligram of Ativan every two weeks is not going to make an abuser of you. It's just going to allow you to enjoy telling your story. Drink some coffee afterwards; you might get a bit drowsy."

Among her friends, acquaintances, relatives, and enemies, Rafe alone did not try to explain her work to her. He did not accuse her of neurotic self-abnegation; he did not commend her for selfless Christian love. Once he had mentioned that he was glad she was never on call; he was tired of women who wore beepers. He liked to listen to descriptions of guests and volunteers, and sometimes he made a clarifying comment. Mainly, he understood that she had found her *métier*. Like an owner of a flying school. Like a member of the House. Like a fellow who wrote and lectured on ancient madness.

But could they live together, the basement cook and the worldly scholar? She doubted it. When she'd spoken of adding to the Ladle a shelter for a dozen people, with herself as resident manager, his ruddy face with its gold and blue markings took on a careful neutrality. They were in her apartment at the time; she had just finished tuning her instrument with the aid of his stethoscope. They sat hip to hip at the harpsichord, facing different directions—he looking at the window, she at the keyboard—as if the wooden bench were a love seat. "And children; don't you want children?" Rafe inquired. She might take on a couple of hard-to-place kids, she said. "And an ordinary life in an ordinary house?" he asked, blinking at the streetlamp. Their upper arms touched.

She didn't answer right away. Ordinary? She could consider an ordinary life; she might bend her wishes to those of somebody ordinary; she might marry, become pregnant, wear the baby in a sling, continue running the Ladle, forget about the shelter and the unadoptables for the twenty years it took to raise a new citizen. To hold her own infant! But Rafe's frank delight in luxury, his enjoyment of the company of talented and learned and talkative and important people . . . "Well?" he prompted, smiling, looking now at her.

"Your life isn't ordinary," she said.

"I would pare it down some," he said.

"Would you serve as co–resident manager of a shelter?"

"No."

Neither spoke. After a while Donna played Scarlatti. Raphael told her that when he closed his eyes he could swear he was listening to Ralph Kirkpatrick.

Occasionally Donna fooled around at the Ladle's upright piano. Usually she was too busy. Sometimes the guests used the piano. Most couldn't manage more than "Chopsticks" or "The Merry Farmer"; but there was one woman with an extensive repertoire of show tunes and jazz. She claimed to have performed with a well-known band, and Donna believed her. She had a large port-wine stain on her cheek. Today she had been seated at the piano since after breakfast, playing "My Funny Valentine" and other tunes of the season. She was rendering "My Heart Stood Still" now, a nice variation with the melody in the left hand and the right moving nimbly through broken chords.

". . . the little cat ran away from me," Lily was saying to Donna, who had sat down beside her. "I left some food in the hall, and it got eaten, but I don't know if that cat ate it or some other cat ate it."

Lily was in danger of eviction from her housing project because of the many cats she kept in her one-room apartment. "You wouldn't believe the stench," another guest had told Donna.

"Beth and one of the volunteers have offered to help you do your spring cleaning," Donna reminded her now.

"It's not spring yet," said Lily.

"You might have less trouble with the superintendent."

"It's not spring yet."

"Whenever you're ready," said Donna. The piano player was ringing chromatic changes on "With a Song in My Heart." Donna glanced at the next table. Bitsy was dressed in various shades of red: magenta shorts over pink tights, a coral blouse, a red ribbon in her hair. Valentine's Day was hard on these women. The lesbians were louder than usual. The Puerto Rican girl was gorgeous as always, her hair shining. She had washed it in a bathroom sink before breakfast; women had to make appointments for shampoos as if the Ladle were a salon. Now she was leafing through a fashion magazine, the sack of belongings under her chair tied loosely to her ankle. She was no more than eighteen. It was hard to believe from her appearance that she slept on the streets three seasons a year—although she, unlike Nellie, was willing to go to a shelter when the weather dropped below thirty. Nellie never went to a shelter; the showers terrified her.

Donna excused herself to Lily and went into the kitchen. An efficient volunteer was directing the food preparation. Thank heaven for volunteerism, Donna thought, for about the thousandth time. Recently she had made the mistake of thinking it aloud, in Josie's presence. "Thank heaven indeed, and damn its current devaluation," Josie instantly began. Did she keep these orations stored up until an opportune moment? "Who visits the sick nowadays?" Josie rhetorically continued. "Nobody. Feminism has a lot to answer for. All over the joint we see dispirited lady lawyers who should be teaching nursery school, for society's sake as well as their own. I should know; Stuyvesant and I are the parents of two of them. And nobody gets properly rested anymore. Greed comes from lack of sleep, I'm convinced. Give me a grant and I'll do the research to prove it."

"Consider yourself granted," Donna had wearily said, and put her hand on the telephone to call People's Pantry.

"For all I mock you, Donna, you are the true New Woman. The postfeminist. Doing the work at hand. Don't you agree?"

To Donna, feminism was as irrelevant as righteousness. "Absolootle," she said, and did pick up the phone.

That was last week, Wednesday, Josie's day. People's Pantry had delivered potatoes and carrots and hamburger meat and bruised apples on Friday. Was anybody making applesauce today? The efficient volunteer told her that since the ovens were free this morning—hamburger soup was a top-of-the-stove dish—the workers were making apple crisp instead. "I can smell it," smiled Donna.

Nellie was back at the medicine chest. "Aspirin." When Donna asked if she had a headache, Nellie didn't respond. "Aspirin isn't good for a stomachache," Donna began. Nellie held out her palm. Donna hesitated, then shook two aspirin onto that dark gray surface. Four other women surged into the place that Nellie had vacated, one of them pointedly holding her nose.

By the time she had finished doling out calcium, hair conditioner, and laxatives, lunch was ready. The Ladle served the women at their tables, as if they were restaurant patrons. A vase of flowers beautified each table. Once the food was served, Donna and Beth sat down with their guests, as did some of the volunteers. Others preferred to remain in stiff attendance in the kitchen.

And by the time lunch was over (the apple crisp was a triumph), it was time for the visit of the housing advocate (she saw people in Donna's little office) and the nurse (she saw people in one corner of the kitchen, more or less screened off. Bitsy liked to peek). A social worker sometimes dropped by too, a warm-hearted, deep-breasted person whom Donna loved; but her services were rarely used. "They don't trust my kind," she said without rancor. Meanwhile, Free Food made a delivery, as did Yesterday's Bread. The third staff member, Pamela, arrived from one of her mendicant tours with a donated set of restaurant silverware (spoons vanished daily, despite Donna's pleadings) and four folding cots, wonderful for hangovers. Pamela walked in just as Vera, a steady guest, was giving vent to her daily hysterics. The CIA was following her again. They knew her name meant Truth, and they meant to destroy her. Donna sat with Vera for a while, listening; then Pam took over. It was almost three. The volunteers had mopped the dining room and put away the dishes. The women were leaving. Hard to send them out into the slush, but at least it wasn't snowing, and the church insisted on repossessing its basement in the late afternoons. Donna was beginning to clean the kitchen stove, and had just stolen a look at Raphael's rubies, when a scream came from the dining room. She bounded out, stuffing the ring back into her pocket. The scream came from the Puerto Rican girl. She was standing in the center of the dining room next to one of the beribboned posts. Her sack of belongings was still attached to her ankle. Her head was thrown backward, her elbows were raised, her long fingers sought each other in her wealth of hair, and she was shrieking.

They soothed her—Donna, Pam, and Vera. After a while she was again seated, giving them an earful of her woes. How mother beat her. How she ran to aunt. Aunt's boyfriend a not-nice man. Not an easy country to get along in, this one, if you have no settled home, if you need, oh, thirty, forty thousand to live a decent life. Didn't like her winter assignment, visiting shelters. Would you like such work? she demanded suddenly of Pam. Would you like dragging your body from place to place, lining up for a bed, never able to let your things out of your sight, always afraid of thieves and insults, no way out, no way out . . . *Would you?* She was shrieking again.

"I wouldn't like it at all," said Pam.

The girl looked at Donna next.

"I wouldn't like it at all."

At Vera, who lived that life.

"Not at all," said Vera.

And the girl turned regal again. She shouldered her sack and marched out in her handsome black cape, only the men's socks and decaying sandals indicating that she might not be traveling on the fast track. The three women watched her leave.

"Borderline psychosis," diagnosed Vera. "Somebody should try Thorazine on her. Shall I do the toilets?"

"Queenie did them today," said Donna. Queenie was another guest.

"Then I'll be off," said Vera.

Pamela and Beth finished washing the kitchen floor, and then they too left. Donna had only two trash barrels to empty and a few bills to pay. Before she settled down at her desk, she decided to treat herself to one more look at the ring.

But the ring was gone.

But it couldn't be gone.

But it was gone.

She stood up, very tall, very straight, and lifted her chin. As if the thought of Rafe's gift had just occurred to her, as if she wanted to sneak up on it unawares, she lowered her thumb into the long narrow front pocket of her jeans while continuing to direct her smile toward the ceiling. Her thumb searched for the treasure. No treasure. Lowered her index finger and her middle finger in turn. Searched the outer pocket, the side pockets, the back pockets, searched the pocket of her striped apron, which she had already hung up.

Searched the kitchen floor. Searched on hands and knees, then on stomach. Searched the other floors. The tiny office. The bathroom. Storage. The basket of dirty tablecloths.

Her heart leaped up when she saw the two trash barrels near the door, waiting to be taken out to the alley. Thank goodness their contents weren't yet in the Dumpster. She put on rubber gloves and began to lift things out of one trash barrel, examine them, and put them into an empty garbage bag. Slowly, very slowly. A crumpled-up bloody Kleenex might not be what it seemed. Nor a soggy mess of Cheerios and yogurt. Nor a broken glass. Why had three perfectly good forks been thrown in here? She set them aside. And why that misshapen plastic ashtray? Disturbing. She drew out, slowly, attentively, too absorbed in the task to notice her own disgust, the rest of the garbage, piece by dripping piece.

An hour and a half later the contents of the first barrel had been transferred to the plastic bag and the contents of the second barrel had been transferred to the first barrel. Donna lugged the mess to the Dumpster and threw it all in.

There was nowhere else to look. The ring had disappeared. It had fallen out of her pocket after one of her childish peeks, and it had been picked up by one of the guests, who would pawn it or peddle it or give it away or lose it or toss it through a sidewalk grate.

Donna went home. She heated Spaghettios for supper. She telephoned her great-aunt in Connecticut and talked for a while. She received two calls: one from the fund-raising chairman of the Ladle, who shared some grandiose plans for a benefit auction; the other from an old friend whose husband was leaving her. Then she undressed—and experienced an upsurge of joy when she realized that she had not yet searched her sneakers. But the ring wasn't there. She lay down on her mattress.

She had trouble falling asleep. She was worried about Raphael. For all his tolerance, he would be dismayed by her carelessness. He would be hurt. She wondered how she could ease the hurt. Perhaps she could live with him for a while—walk to the Ladle from his home instead of hers, scramble eggs for two, warm those damned towels. Sit in his living room and listen to the witticisms of aging intellectuals. His piano needed tuning.

And she needed rest. She reached under her mattress and found the vial of Ativan and teased out two tablets and swallowed them without water, without even opening her eyes, like a suburban wife accustomed to dealing with marital woes.

Raphael, meanwhile, like a philandering husband, sat at his hotel bar and flirted with a pediatrician from Maryland, in town for a conference. She was a widow. Her sons were in college. Crinkle-eyed, handsome, confident, warm, flexible—he could hear his friends and his children piling on the praise. She was a trustee of her temple, and was more or less familiar with the prophets. She laughed mellowly when he told her about almost leaving the plane ticket in his bedroom. (He didn't mention the ring.) What a candidate for marriage! She could take a supervisory job in a Boston teaching hospital. Nice brown eyes she had. And such a bosom, adorned with a topaz on a chain . . .

He paid for their drinks and wished her good night. He slipped off his stool and walked swiftly out of the bar. Perhaps she would think that a fever had gripped his bowels, and in a way she would be right, only it was passion that was shaking him, and what it was shaking was his heart; he was seized by longing for the skinny, uncompromising spinster who right now was probably giving succor if not a night's lodging to some derelict woman.

He leaned against the wall of the elevator and pushed the button for his floor. He would make Donna an offer. He would suggest that they live together in one of the brick row houses not far from the Ladle. He would take a supervisory position in a Boston teaching hospital. He would continue his out-of-town lecturing, but only once a month. He would serve as primary housekeeper and child-care provider. Hadn't he brought up his first three children, and splendidly? She knew that. He did not believe in that convenient fiction quality time; he believed in time, lots of it. She knew that, too. Did she know how much he loved her? "I'm pregnant," he imagined himself announcing. Then she'd know.

Raphael slept. Donna slept. Nellie slept too, on the floor in the chair room, waking up every few hours to its dull, dark warmth. No headlights. No shelter vans out looking for people, no police cruisers. At about four she woke up for good and crept out of her hiding place. The dining room was as dark as the chair room, but in the kitchen there was a bit of light– some from a high window partly blocked with snow, and some from the pilot light in the stove, which could be seen through a hole in the cast iron. With the aid of that blue flame, her indifferent eyes saw the gleam of an object caught in the cuff of the stove, where it had landed after bouncing on the floor, when Donna dropped it, when the Puerto Rican girl screamed.

Nellie bent to pick up the glitter. She took it to the place under the window. The sky had lightened further. The thing was red, in the shape of a heart. She put it into her mouth. She spat it out. She saw that it was a ring. It reminded her of something—a gift in a Crackerjack box that one of her Mummas had let her keep. The thought of that Mumma made her feel sick. The bitch had worn an apron. Here was an apron, hanging. She thrust the thing into its pocket. Was that noise the janitor? No, not yet, just a truck on the street. She would wait in the bathroom until she heard the janitor come in, fuckin' sonofabitch, then she'd go out, she'd go, all right she'd go.

Donna was at work by seven. She took the apron from its hook by the stove and put it on, and felt the ring. Instantly, as if its touch did have magic, she fell to her knees. She was still on her knees when Josie came in ten minutes later. "Good God," said Josie, squatting beside the sobbing woman, enfolding her, stroking Donna's cheek with her birdlike beak. "What happened, Donna? You haven't been raped, have you? Speak to me, Donna! Shall I call the police?"

Donna shook her head and regained enough command to show her cousin the ring and tell its recent history. "It must have been in the apron all the time, only in my panic I couldn't find it. I think I was out of my mind. Straining all the garbage," she gulped. "You should have seen me."

They had drawn away from each other, though both were still kneeling on the floor in front of the black stove. "So you lost your boyfriend's trinket, and you found your boyfriend's trinket," Josie summed up. She too had regained her composure, and Donna braced herself for what would certainly come next: Don't you know that you lost your real heart some time ago? But her kinswoman said only: "'The greatest griefs are those we cause ourselves.' That's from Shakespeare."

It was from Sophocles, but Donna kept her mouth shut. He would get a kick out of the choric Josie, Rafe would: dear man, her man, her heart's desire.

CHARITY

~~~~~~~~~~~~~~~~~~~~~~~~~~~~~~~~

"I'm invited to a bat mitzvah," said Donna.

"Lovely. What's a bat mitzvah?" said Mag.

Silence. Mag moved her mop back and forth.

"A ceremony of initiation for a Jewish child," Donna said at last.

"And you a lamb of Christ. So, whose ceremony of whatever?"

"Bluma's granddaughter. You know Bluma, she volunteers on Thursdays."

"I do. Painted yellow hair, painted purple mouth. A wide lady."

Silence again. Donna's Ladle made a point of discouraging antisocial behavior—drinking, shooting up, stealing, catty remarks.

"Would *wide* be a bad word, now? Perhaps I intended a compliment." Mag raised her mop and shook it playfully at Donna. Drops of water fell onto the bathroom floor.

Donna had just finished scrubbing the toilets. She was leaning against a sink. She looked down at Mag's soapy globules mottling a linoleum so cracked that in some places it revealed its brown interior.

"Bluma *is* wide," Donna admitted.

"Donna's Ladle needs all the help it can get," said Mag kindly.

We certainly do, Donna thought; but Bluma had an eccentric way of helping. She always began her stint by planting herself halfway between oven and cutting counter. Workers wanting to get by had to brush her rump with theirs or return her curly smile nose to nose. Meanwhile, Bluma announced family triumphs to anyone who'd listen. Sooner or later she managed to peel a few potatoes and chop a few onions. She was an expert at carrot spirals. Sometimes she wandered into the dining room and sat with one of the guests. A conversation began. Bluma took on most of its burden; that was evident from the expression on the listener's face—stony or spacy or flat-out asleep.

Donna turned to the sinks. She scrubbed them. She polished the mirror. Behind her Mag was finishing the floors. "Did you see Olive today?" Donna asked through the mirror.

"I did. Poor soul."

Olive, an elderly guest, suffered from advanced skin cancer. In some places her skin was peeling away, in others it was growing rough little tags. Red nuggets were embedded here and there.

Mag mopped. "I'm taking Olive out to coffee when I'm done."

"Bless you," Donna said.

She went into her windowless office, which had been knocked together in one corner of the furnace room. Sometimes in the winter her cubicle got so hot that, after the others had left, she took off her shirt and worked in her bra, flouting the decorum she'd been raised to respect. Rafe, finding her in this attire on a January evening, had likened her to a Magritte: shocking so as to instruct. Then he'd asked her to put on her shirt. A psychiatrist and a scholar of ancient madness, *he* was subject to attacks of seemliness.

But on this Monday in July, the basement was cool, and Donna kept her clothes on. She sat at her desk and picked up the volunteer schedule for next week. There was one hole, on Tuesday afternoon—nobody had signed for clean-up—but perhaps she could rope in that late-night radio person, what's-her-name, available for emergencies.

What's-her-name usually mentioned the Ladle on the show afterward: nice publicity for the shoestring operation.

The staff appreciated emergency workers like the radio person. They loved the dozen or so faithfuls, women who turned up for the whole day, always the same day, once a week, week after week after week. Mag labored through cruel hangovers, doing whatever had to be done. Others were fussy, so the staff fit the task to the foible. One gaunt woman wanted only to scrub pots. Another liked to play therapist, roiling people up, encouraging them to conflate inventions and dreams and fancies and wishes and then call the mix memory. There was an activist forever circulating petitions to the governor of Massachusetts that no one read though everyone signed.

The evening Rafe found her in her bra he read through the master list of volunteers.

"Are you looking for people you know?" she wondered, buttoning her blouse.

"I'm looking for Jewish names; it's a Jewish tic," he said. "There aren't many. Bluma Markoff, Edna Pearl, Marjorie Weinstein. The others are Yankee or Irish."

"Edna Pearl is a Baptist woman of color."

"Oh. Well, Jews are taking care of their fellow Jews, here and in Israel, as maybe we should."

"Really? 'I am not an Athenian nor a Greek, but a citizen of the world,'" she said, using his beloved Socrates against him. Then she added in a softer voice that Jewish contributions of money to the Ladle were numerous, and that Jewish pocketbooks were deep.

August was always unkind to the Ladle's guests. Pavements cracked with heat. Afternoons were as long as weeks. Summer was the worst season for panhandling—it took cold weather to warm people's hearts. "Help the needy, don't be greedy," called out one of the Ladle's guests on Strawbridge Boulevard, shaking a paper cup. Few passersby responded. "Get cancer," she yelled at their backs. Donna suggested that the parting shot wasn't helpful. "When I want your fucking advice, Donna, I'll phone you from my slab."

One Thursday just after midnight there was a blackout affecting half the town. When Donna opened up at seven-thirty she found that the Ladle's freezer was more or less working. But the milk in the refrigerator had soured and the cottage cheese meant for lasagna had turned yellow. She sent Lisa, a teenage volunteer with Down's syndrome, out to buy milk. In the pale light from the high basement windows, Lisa's underslung face and mild eyes looked full of wisdom. But as soon as the girl left, Donna realized that new purchases would soon sour, too; she was relieved when Lisa returned with boxes of powdered milk, not cartons of fresh.

Breakfast was murky that morning. At eleven the electricity still wasn't restored. Donna called the local pizza parlor, whose ovens used gas. She ordered sixty pizzas and wrote a check on the emergency account. The truck came an hour later. The driver refused the money. And so the most-praised and least expensive lunch of the summer was enjoyed by candlelight; when the power did rush on, the ceiling fluorescence revealed eight tables of dreamy women, telling tales as if around campfires, feasting on pizza and soft ice cream and, at the table farthest from the kitchen, on beer. Under cover of darkness one mischievous guest had brought in a six-pack.

Some parts of Olive's suddenly illuminated face now had a petal whiteness. She blinked at Donna. "I'll be visiting my daughter soon."

She had never before mentioned a daughter. Donna kept her own face neutral.

"Wonderful!" said Bluma. "*My* daughter's daughter is about to become bat mitzvah." She brought her chair closer to Olive. She herself looked less garish than usual because so many other people wore clown's make-up too—tomato sauce lipstick, ice cream beards, and a few Budweiser mustaches.

The calligraphic envelope arrived on the first Saturday in September. It was too big for Donna's mailbox; the postman propped it against the vestibule wall, where Donna found it after an early morning bike ride. *Ms. Donna Crowninshield,* the envelope began. Rafe's name was underneath hers, augmented by both title and degree: *Doctor Raphael Bazelon M.D.*

Rafe, clad only in briefs, was drinking coffee by the open window. Donna gave him his newspaper, then opened the envelope. The card within had been formed by layering three heavy blue papers, Wedgwood over cobalt over an Aegean silver. The letters of the words *Bat Mitzvah* had been cut out of the Wedgwood, revealing the cobalt; the letters of the celebrant's name had been cut out of both Wedgwood and cobalt, revealing the silver. Donna had never before received so elaborate a construction. She estimated its cost at five dollars.

"There are economies of scale," Rafe mumbled. "And to your silent question, the answer is no. My children's invitations were black script on ivory vellum." He held the creation at arm's length, though he was wearing his reading glasses. "Do we have to?"

"I've sort of said yes. But no, we don't have to. Bluma is . . . not a treasure."

"Well, then." But he didn't put the card down; just kept his eyes on Donna, as if a scholarly gaze could quench the fire that leaped between them. She bent forward and kissed the inside of his elbow.

Later, head on his chest, ankles rubbing his, she remarked to the bedroom window that she had reached the age of thirty-five without ever attending a bat mitzvah or even a bar mitzvah. If she were going to end up married to a Jew, perhaps she should seize this opportunity . . .

She felt his heart whirring like a slot machine. The tumblers fell into joyous repose. "I'll save the date," he said.

The date was the first Saturday in October. During the preceding month Olive's oncologist summoned her to the hospital—an organ was now affected with disease. Each Thursday, Bluma left as usual before cleanup; these days she walked out consulting a fluttering list of things to do. Two guests returned unexpectedly from California. They had set off in June—half the clientele at the Ladle had thrown confetti at the departing bus. Now each wore bruises inflicted by the other.

New volunteers recruited themselves, filled with the ardor of autumn. Old volunteers returned—most of them. Some had burnt out or worked off their privilege or exhausted their penance or taken regular jobs. Mag swabbed the floors Monday after Monday. When the cleaning was done, she and Donna often went to the park for a cigarette. One afternoon they took the trolley to the hospital. Olive was hooked up to an IV, her gray eyes translucent in her shredded face. "Lord, Lord, my dear friends," was all she said, though she said it more than once. She slept, opened her eyes, smiled, slept again. Donna and Mag sat with her until they had to yield their place to a priest in cassock and sneakers.

On the morning of the bat mitzvah the gilded dome of the synagogue seemed to glow. Rafe guided Donna up a flight of broad stairs to the open doors of the sanctuary. Where had he dug up that flamingo tie? His pale gold hair foamed in the sun. Donna was wearing a putty dress with a matching cartwheel hat. "You draw eyes, the two of you"— she could hear Mag saying it, even though Mag hadn't seen them. Mag was probably sleeping off her Friday binge at her sister's house in Dorchester. She would be sobered up by tomorrow, for Olive's funeral.

In the vestibule Rafe picked up a black skullcap and flattened the suds of his hair. They found seats near the front. The service had apparently begun, though people were still streaming into the sanctuary behind them. There would be a crowd, all right—several hundred, Bluma had said—but they would fill only the front of this tremendous hall, which accommodated a thousand families during the High Holy Days. Bluma had told her that, too.

A stout girl in a short dotted dress sat in one of the chairs on the stage—the bima, Rafe called it last night when he sketched out the proceedings for Donna. The child had a headful of yellow curls. Perhaps Bluma had once really been blond; perhaps she dyed her hair in memory of past glory. Now Donna caught sight of Bluma in the second row. Her radiant coiffure was topped with a black satin pouf. A shrunken woman sat at her side—her mother, Donna knew. Bluma's mother wore a hat covered with silk hydrangeas.

The service went on, mostly in English. The responsive prayers repeated themselves. Rafe had told her that the English translation weakened the rough and authoritative Hebrew. That didn't matter, Donna thought; these people did not have to plead for deliverance. They had already been brought from bondage.

"The congregation will rise," said the rabbi, often. "The congregation may be seated," he said, just as often. Sometimes Bluma's mother rose so slowly that by the time she was up everybody else was down again. She stood alone for an unembarrassed moment, then shakily the figure in the bright blue hat lowered herself into the crowd.

When the chanting was in Hebrew, phlegmy consonants bubbled from Rafe's throat, behind the knot of his outrageous tie. Such strong colors burned in this holy place—Rafe's tie, Bluma's hair, the citrus brilliance of stained glass, an orange carpet flaming down the aisles and across the bima. Donna felt conspicuous in her colorlessness: a drab Christian, not yet saved.

The Law was brought out of the ark, producing a mild heave of excitement. The congregation rose without prompting. The rabbi and the cantor and some elders marched with the scrolls down one orange aisle and across the rear and up the center. The procession approached Donna's row; everyone around her turned, as if toward a bride. Rafe reached his prayer book across three people and touched the Torah with its spine. Paganly, he brought the book to his lips.

The scroll and its bearers returned to the bima, and at last narration took over, though in Hebrew, not English. The granddaughter's task was to read this week's portion of Torah, Rafe had explained. Members of the family would be called up to recite prayers. After each prayer the celebrant would read a few sentences. When her portion was completed she would chant another piece of Scripture, not Torah. Then she would present a brief commentary in English. The rabbi would praise her. More prayers would follow, including one for mourners, the Kaddish. "And finally, *Shabbat shalom,* we'll all have a drink," Rafe wound up.

"And lunch," said Donna. "Lunch is my middle name."

"We'll be seated at the Odd People's table," Rafe predicted. "Our companions will be the black maid and her consort, and the middle school science teacher and his wife, and half a dozen other misfits. That at least will be fun."

Donna knew better from Bluma. They were to feast at the table of dignitaries, which included an under-secretary of the interior, husband to some cousin. She kept this disagreeable news to herself.

Everything now went as Rafe had said—prayer and reading, prayer and reading. Bluma, the only grandparent, read the blessing in her confident rasp. The square-faced child soldiered on.

"How's she doing?" Donna whispered to Rafe.

"Fine. Sooner or later she'll smile. A good kid."

And when the good kid came to chant the non-Torah part, her pleasing voice transcended the gloomy melody. She chanted and chanted. At last the tune changed, and the words became familiar even to Donna—some version of the blessing that was repeated so often. A murmur rippled across the congregation.

The young lady produced a small sheaf of papers and began to talk in English. Donna slouched against the back of the pew. Her cartwheel tipped forward.

"*Tsdekah.*" More Hebrew? Donna straightened. "*Tsdekah* has many meanings," said the girl. "It means doing the right thing. It means simple charity, putting money into a person's hands. It means generosity toward our own Jewish institutions. It means paying attention to what matters to other people, too, who may be different from us, but . . ."

Not diversity *again*, Donna silently groaned; may sweet Jesus protect her from words that already put her to sleep at grant makers' workshops. Empowerment, mission: today's garbagespeak.

". . . the best example I know of *tsdekah* is my grandmother, Bluma Markoff. Grandma Bluma, like dear Great-grandma Anna before her, runs our family with a velvet hand. She praises us when we are ordinary, and she consoles us when we don't know we're down." There was a wave of friendly laughter. Donna peered through a grove of shoulders until she could see Bluma's smiling profile. "What else does Grandma Bluma do? One day a week, every week, for five years now, Grandma Bluma takes herself to Donna's Soup Kitchen, a facility for poor women. She chops, she scrapes, she boils, she ladles; she serves, she clears, she scrubs, she mops." Pause, possibly from exhaustion. "And she gets to know these wretched women." Pause, probably for effect. "And they rise up and call her blessed."

Rafe's forehead was pink and his cheeks pinker. Face, tie . . . what a palette. Donna touched his arm, hoping to staunch the rush of bitter embarrassment. *Shalom,* she whispered.

But she too was seething. Seven years ago when she had opened the Ladle, she had served lunch only twice a week, with the help of a pair of retired schoolteachers and a boy who came in after school to wash the floors. Now the schoolteachers were dead and Joe was a seminarian and the Ladle was, according to its most recent award, an enterprise "scraping by on individual contributions and private grants, uninquisitive, unbureaucratic: a true community." Yes; all of them, Mag and Lisa and Olive and everybody, chopping, and singing at the piano, and collaborating on heroic biographies, and plunging finicky toilets. Let the community be called blessed—not wide, brazen Bluma.

"Grandma Bluma is not modest," admitted the bat mitzvah, lifting her shoulders. Her eyes met Donna's, an exchange unmediated by coiffures and yarmulkes—why did nothing interfere with this stare of confrontation? Then Donna realized that she herself was on her feet. Quickly she adjusted her hat. She became aware of a figure materializing at her right, slowly—reluctantly, perhaps. Rafe was standing beside her.

"Modesty is a low virtue, if you ask me," the celebrant went on. Was Pride then a high calling? "Grandma's tales have inspired me," pleaded the girl. Bluma, with a confused gurgle, took this tribute as an invitation. She rose. The assembly held its collective breath. The blue flowers of the great-grandmother's hat bobbed unsteadily into view. "Mama, you don't have to . . ." whispered Bluma loudly. "Is it Kaddish already?" asked an old man in the rear.

The girl on the bima laughed. Her shoulders relaxed. She stifled the laugh, but a broad grin remained. "My dear friends," she said, "thank you everybody for everything. The congregation may be seated."

Bluma, Donna, and Rafe immediately sat. The old woman took her time about it. The rabbi blessed the bat mitzvah. Donna looked intently at her lap, and did not look up again, and did not stand again. "*Mazel tov,*" said Rafe, leaning down to kiss her. "It's over."

Ten minutes later, in a corner of the reception room, he touched her champagne glass with his. "Donna, may I ask . . . were we rising to bear witness against Bluma?"

". . . we were rising in affirmation. *Sedekah,* that's how you say it?"

"T, S, as in nuts. We were affirming grandiosity?"

"*Tsdekah.* The fund-raisers' next buzzword."

"We were affirming lies?" he insisted.

"Bluma does show up," Donna reminded him. "I affirm lies every day of the week," she added. Then she drank the champagne, all of it, fast, thinking helplessly of Olive's flayed face, and the soul that had shone so blindingly from its ruins.

DOROTHEA

By the time the left-most toilet in the ladies' room had completely ceased to function, all three members of the staff of Donna's Ladle had taken a hand in trying to fix it. Some of the guests offered advice, too. Since the Ladle served breakfast and lunch to women five days a week, the bathrooms were important. The ladies' room had three stalls; often all were occupied at once. The men's room, commandeered by the Ladle during its open hours, had one stall. It also had a urinal, which was occasionally used—against the advice of staff—for brushing teeth.

Each of the toilets was in the habit of overflowing. The incident usually occurred in the middle of the morning, and one of the guests would inform one of the three staff members. (It was understood that an overflowing toilet was not the business of volunteers.) Roxanne often elected herself to do the reporting. She had a strong attachment to Donna's Ladle; she'd shown up on the day of its opening, seven years earlier, looking much the same as she looked now: fanged, whiskered, dressed in layers of ragged clothing. One of her eyes was blind. She smoked a yellow pipe. Roxanne removed the pipe from her mouth only to eat or to announce current events to the air around her. "Blizzard," she'd proclaim. "Rats in the alley." "War." To tell of a flood in the bathroom, "toilet" was all she needed to say, though she did need to say it directly to a person—to Donna, so calm and tall, or to sturdy Pamela, or to roly-poly Beth.

Then Donna or Pam or Beth would trundle a mop and a pail into the bathroom. Roxanne, her task done, would sit down at one of the dining tables and resume breakfast. But perhaps little Bitsy, strutting like a majorette, or Karin, dreadlocks awhirl, would decide to be helpful, would hunt up the Out of Order—*Please* Do Not Use sign and tape it to the door of the disabled stall. Meanwhile, the staff member would mop up the mess. Then she'd swab the floor a second time with water and detergent. Then she'd resume her usual duties. As soon as possible, she'd return, gauntleted in rubber, to correct the problem—to remove the obstruction, sluice, plunge, often to gag.

That was the usual procedure. But today, quite early in the morning, the left-most toilet was acknowledged to be entirely beyond anyone's competence to repair. It could not be flushed; it wouldn't even overflow. Donna had fooled around with the tank, but to no avail. Pam's snake had reached but had not been able to penetrate the obstruction within the outflow pipe. And Beth, who could interpose her round body between two warring women, who could soft-talk a guest into repocketing a knife, shook her curly head in surrender. So Donna called the pro bono plumber, who said he'd get over as soon as he could—Friday was his best guess.

"It's Monday, Frank!"

"Darlin'. I'm booked solid. And you've got three other commodes, me love."

The Out of Order sign was already in place. Donna and Pam and Beth returned to their various tasks, praying that the warning would be heeded.

Probably only a few guests ignored the sign. Perhaps they were impelled by mischief, perhaps by desperate need, perhaps by private fury. At any rate, at three o'clock, after the last guest had left, Donna and Pam and Beth were confronted with a full, reeking toilet bowl whose contents they had to transfer by means of empty cottage cheese cartons to the neighboring toilet. They cleaned the bowl as best they could with warm water and bleach. Despite a stringent supplies budget, they threw the gloves and sponges they'd used into the trash.

"Now we have to screw the door closed," said Donna.

Such work fell to the handy Pamela. Pam carried her toolbox into the stall. She locked herself in and drilled a hole next to the lock and another hole into a small bar of metal. She placed the metal bar next to the bolt of the lock, jamming it. She screwed the metal bar to the door; Donna, on the outside, held the nut in place. Then Pamela slid the toolbox under the door and wriggled after it on her stomach.

Donna, leaning against the sink with her arms folded, watched Pam play marine. Her large eyes were thoughtful. "If you can do that, half of our guests can do it too," she said. "The Out of Order sign was apparently a challenge. A locked door might be a challenge, too."

Pam, still belly-down on the linoleum, consulted Donna's Reeboks. "Let's put a pair of boots in front of the toilet," she suggested. "As if somebody were on the pot. The women don't like rules, but they do respect privacy."

They found Beth in the back closet, sorting a pile of donated clothing. She had already discarded a pair of badly ripped galoshes. "People use us as a rubbish barrel," she complained.

Donna ran off to the ladies' room waving the galoshes. Pam trotted after her. Beth came too, wondering what was up.

Kneeling before the locked stall, Donna managed to reach in and place the boots in a convincing position, one slightly in front of the other. But, empty and ripped, they kept falling over. "We'll have to stuff them with bricks," she muttered.

"No," said Beth. "Let's give them feet and legs."

"A whole bod!" said Pam.

Donna, still on hands and knees, grinned over her shoulder at her inspired staff.

And so three fatigued young women—who prided themselves on their practicality, who had more work to do that week than they could get done in a month, whose personal lives needed attention (Donna was six weeks pregnant, Pam's companion seemed to be turning her hot eyes toward somebody new, Beth's mother had cancer)—recklessly postponed their afternoon's commitments and undertook to construct a dummy.

They assembled a wardrobe from the donated clothing. They chose a full skirt in houndstooth check and a jacket of herringbone tweed. They found a threadbare Burberry muffler and a man's fedora. They brought these things into the vestibule of the ladies' room along with a few items from their pantry.

"Somebody could use this hat," said Beth, caressing the brim.

"Dorothea will give it back," said Donna.

"Dorothea?" mumbled Pam. One corner of her mouth held safety pins; she was stuffing a trash bag with a number of other trash bags. This was to be the prototype's trunk. Its bottom was weighted with an eight-pound can of sauerkraut. "Dorothea Dix?" Pam had studied social reform in college.

"Sure," said Donna, who had in fact been thinking of Dorothea Casaubon, in *Middlemarch*.

"My uncle's English grandmother was named Dorothea," said Beth. "She was a batty bluestocking. Chained herself to fences and stuff. Do you like this face?"

She had been stitching features onto the seat of a pair of panty hose, extra-large. Thin red lips, staring blue eyes.

"Too generic," objected Pam.

"Try eyebrows," Donna suggested.

Beth said she'd find some rags to plump out the face. Maybe in three dimensions . . .

"We should give Dorothea something to read," said Pam. She had fastened the last of the safety pins, and she now created a waist with a piece of string. Then she went off to raid the Ladle's bookshelf for a Regency romance. But she came back with volume one of *The History of the Peloponnesian War,* in large type. "It'll stay open on her lap," she said.

Pam and Donna dressed the torso in skirt and jacket. They rounded the jacket's arms with crumpled newspapers, and they attached green mittens to the cuffs. They laid Dorothea, still headless and legless, on the ladies' room's scabby floor. Pam crawled into the locked stall. Donna gently pushed the dummy under the door, then slid in herself, on her back, protecting her unborn child.

Beth returned, holding something under her arm. She was too fat to wriggle after her colleagues into the stall, and anyway there wasn't room for another person. So she stood on the adjoining toilet and watched over the partition as Pam and Donna seated Dorothea and made sure that the tweed skirt hung over the tops of the boots (each now steadied with a thirty-two-ounce Campbell's Pork 'n Beans).

"She doesn't need legs," Pam noted.

Dorothea's rump of sauerkraut held her in place on the turned-down toilet lid. A broken broomstick stiffened her back. Her mittens rested on Thucydides, open to Pericles' funeral oration. "How's the face coming?" said Donna.

"You tell me," said Beth. She raised a flesh-colored object above the partition.

Beth had constructed a skull inside the embroidered panty hose. She had used an empty plastic tub for the forehead, a saltshaker for the nose, and a round cork cutting board for the lower jaw. She had fleshed out this makeshift head with bits of flannel and terry cloth. The visage that resulted was no longer generic. It was specific and horrible. The eyes were sunken beneath the rounded brow. The nose was off center, as if struck too often. The scarlet lips were sullen. A blob of blue eye shadow on one cheek provided a bruise. Instead of a scalp and hair, though, the rim of the plastic container rose above the waistband of the panty hose. Instead of a neck, two limp nylon legs hung below the jutting jaw.

"Fantastic," said Donna.

Pamela signified her approval with a salute. She took the creation from Beth and settled it onto Dorothea's torso and pinned it in place. She taped silver scouring pads to the brow and covered the empty brain with the fedora. Donna turned the hat brim down and the jacket collar up. She draped the Burberry over the shoulders.

Then Pam slid out—feet first this time, and on her back. Donna followed. Beth stepped from her perch. She and Pam went off to unload the last batch of crockery from the dishwasher. Donna lay on the floor for a minute, staring at the bulb that hung from the ceiling. Then she rolled over, stood, stumbled into the middle stall, and threw up. She joined Pam and Beth in the kitchen. They turned out all the lights and went home.

The next day, they took turns checking on Dorothea, or at least on Dorothea's feet. They felt a collective remorse—for their disrespect, for their insensitivity, for the fun they'd had. Donna knew that as director of the Ladle she bore most of the responsibility. Beth fretted that the face was so cruel. *These are my friends,* she thought, looking at the outcasts milling around the breakfast buffet—some so ragged, some so timid, some so nasty, some whose beauty belied their crazy thoughts. *Why did I insult them?*

Pamela swore at herself for dreaming up the dummy in the first place.

"And suppose somebody finds her?" she whispered to Beth as they were setting up a spare table just before lunch. Foul March weather had brought in even more guests than usual.

"No one will find her." Beth tried to be reassuring.

But Pam continued to worry. Suppose Roxanne were to put her good eye close to the very narrow aperture where stall door met stall; suppose she were to exchange glances with the effigy who might be her sister? Or suppose Vera saw Dorothea? With her hair in a bun and Oxfords on her feet, Vera still looked like the schoolteacher she'd once been. She had requested the next brimmed hat that got donated. How would she feel when she saw that fedora? Bitsy, who liked to accuse the staff of malfeasance (embezzlement and poisoning were recent favorites), would raise her little fist and inveigh against them as usual. But this time Bitsy would be right.

"Dorothea is fine," said Donna late that afternoon, squinting through the slit. "She's learning about Greek burial procedures. But I'm glad that no major donors are coming around this week."

By Wednesday their guilt had diminished, and with it their fear of detection. There was much to distract them. The milk delivery was late. Thursday's ground turkey, thawing, smelled odder than usual. Some petty thefts had occurred: Roxanne's umbrella, the kitchen shears. There was an excessive demand for ice water, but Pam couldn't figure out who was passing around whiskey. Karin was so snap-fingered high that she didn't sit down even to eat; her dreadlocks seemed to be dancing on their own. The toilet in the men's room overflowed. A new volunteer, elderly and very shabby herself, did the mopping and plunging. Donna thanked her gravely, wondering whether she was rich enough to serve on the board.

On Thursday there was another spring storm. The ground turkey seemed to pass muster, so Beth made croquettes. Several women refused even to taste them, and Bitsy threatened to report the Ladle to the commissioner of public health. Donna ignored her first-trimester nausea and ate a large helping of croquettes as an encouraging example. She felt slightly better afterwards. Vera and a new guest sang "April Showers." The ice-water crowd played a noisy game of Hearts. Roxanne didn't want to leave at closing time.

Friday was a beautiful day. But Beth came to work red-eyed. Her mother's cancer had spread. It was now in the bones.

The missing umbrella turned up in the storage room, supposedly off limits to the guests.

"Nothing we can do," said Pam to Donna.

"No. Somebody sneaked in here, maybe took something, left the stolen umbrella as payment. Roxanne will be glad to have it back."

"We're missing a few onions," said Pam. She was peering into one of the barrels, a smile on her odd, snub-nosed face. The love crisis must have passed, thought Donna.

And then it was three o'clock, and the last guest was gone, and the week was over, and Frank the plumber was due in half an hour. Dorothea's boots were still in place. Donna peeked at the mannequin through the aperture. One hand still rested on her book. The other arm hung down, its mitten flat. A cuff of wrinkled newspaper showed at the jacket's wrist. But all else was well—that is, ill: Dorothea under her fedora looked even more battered, bruised, and jaundiced than she had on the day of her creation. Her glasses were broken. Her skirt . . . Glasses?

Pam carried the toolbox as lightly as if it were an attaché case.

"When did you decide she needed glasses?" asked Donna.

"When did I what?" said Pam, taking the screwdriver from the chest and snaking under the door. "Oh, I see. Beth must have . . . Hold the nut with the pliers, Donna, okay?"

She removed the screw and unbarred the lock and opened the door. Then she turned to Dorothea. "The glasses are flattering," she said.

"Did you add those?" said Donna to Beth, who was now standing beside her in front of the sink.

"How?" demanded Beth. "You know I could never squeeze under the door. Why are you accusing me?"

"Easy, easy," soothed Donna. "Somebody must have done it, babes."

Somebody must have. And somebody had also put a pint whiskey bottle, empty, into the right-hand pocket of the jacket. Pam discovered it as she gently frisked the seated Dorothea. And somebody—perhaps a colleague of the first somebody—had slipped a syringe into the left pocket. Pam's clever fingers recognized the needle through the tweed; she put on a rubber glove before teasing it out and dropping it into the bottle. And somebody—perhaps a third conspirator—had highlighted the Periclean line "We make friends by doing good" with a yellow pen.

"What's that in her side?" Beth asked abruptly.

Beneath the peplum of the jacket, the zipper of the skirt gaped open. Somebody had driven the kitchen shears into Dorothea's hip.

In silence they retrieved the jacket and the skirt and the muffler, the glasses and the shears and the book. They carried the head and the body and the pint bottle and the boots out of the basement and up the stone stairs and into the alley. Pam opened the lid of the Dumpster and Donna and Beth laid Dorothea's remains on top of the sacks of garbage. Beth grabbed the hat just before Pam lowered the lid.

They stood together, shivering without their parkas, their hair whipped by the March wind.

"We meant no harm," said Pam after a while.

"They meant no harm, either," said Donna.

"The shears," Beth reminded her friends.

"A symbol," said Donna. "Of the dangers of street life."

"Cigarettes in the breast pocket," said Pam suddenly. "How could we have left them out?"

"Next time," said Donna.

They stared at her. "Next time the scissors will go into a heart," said Pam.

"One of ours," said Beth.

Donna sighed. "What a week."

"Karin's sister took her in again," exclaimed Beth. "I forgot to tell you both."

"We got that grant from the Flaherty Trust," said Donna. "I forgot to tell *you*."

Thus they improvised their way toward recovery. By the time Frank the plumber's truck came rumbling into the alley, they had turned away from the Dumpster and were filing toward the Ladle: Donna first, leaning slightly backwards to compensate for her three-ounce embryo; Pam next, hands in pockets, scraping some damp debris from the side of her sneaker; Beth padding along softly in the rear, the fedora under her arm.

REHEARSALS

Donna's aunt, who was also Josie's aunt, was supplying the flowers for the wedding. Whatever kind they wanted, she said, however many they wanted. Boutonnieres for the men and bouquets for the women, and as much greenery as possible—palms, lilacs, citrus trees in tubs—anything to beautify the thoroughly unattractive locale. "*Must* Donna be married from her soup kitchen?" the aunt husked into the telephone—in her eighth decade, she still had the voice of a femme fatale. "The place is so uncompromisingly a church basement."

"You know our Donna," said Josie. "It's the basement or nowhere. Your flowers will be a big help."

Josie, as organizer of the occasion, next sought out Bucky. Bucky, a faithful volunteer at Donna's Ladle, delivered donated foodstuffs from all over town. He could balance a crate of watermelons on one shoulder.

Bucky authorized himself to provide any necessary carpentry. "You want bleachers, me and my boys we'll give you bleachers," he said, his eyes jumping in his big pirate's face. "A platform? A fount?"

Josie said, "Wouldn't that be nice. But my cousin thrives on bare bones. So just a canopy for the bride and groom and a trellis on the wall to support a few sprays."

Bucky beamed. "Depend on me."

Donna and Raphael insisted on addressing all two hundred envelopes themselves. Starving calligraphers make ends meet by addressing envelopes, Josie mentioned. They ignored the hint. Either Donna or Rafe, and sometimes both, added a personal note to each invitation. Such consumption of time, Josie complained to her husband; you'd never guess they were professionals, neither in their first youth, and both overworked.

One afternoon, two weeks before the wedding, Josie mentioned the rehearsal dinner.

"Rehearsal *dinner?*" said Donna. "We're not even having a rehearsal."

Josie, expecting this response—hoping for it, in fact—then suggested a rehearsal.

The cousins faced each other. They were sorting vegetables in the back storage room of the Ladle. Each wore somebody else's clothing. Over her jeans Donna wore her fiancé's shirt, not tucked in, its tails hanging. This outfit would have been considered a sly announcement if Donna had been keeping mum about her pregnancy. But secrecy hadn't occurred to her; and, anyway, some of the guests at the Ladle had spotted her condition when her period was only a week late. "Womens get a look around the eyes," mused Allie. "Like, you know, ethereal."

At present Donna's large and colorless eyes were glaring at Josie. "A wedding is not a performance."

"That's some shirt," deflected Josie.

The shirt, made by a famous designer, was striped in the dark purples of a Venetian painting. Josie peered closely. "There's a thin stripe of gold, I thought so. It must look wonderful on Rafe."

Donna nodded. Rafe's collection of dark suits and brilliant shirts did look wonderful on him—trim as he was, blond as he still was, fifty-one though he would soon be.

Josie's garment had been borrowed without forethought. The wind blowing through the bulkhead of the Godolphin Unitarian Church had chilled her; she'd plucked a peacoat from the pile of donations. The peacoat once belonged to a large person; Josie was wearing it as a cape. Her head with its persimmon hair did not quite rise above the gaping collar. It was as if a sailor had flung his jacket over a chattering parrot in an attempt to silence it.

The parrot went on. "Quite a shirt, Donna, and your wedding dress is quite a dress. I'm glad Rafe persuaded you to buy that Empire silk." Donna scowled. "You'll look like Madame Récamier. And the attendants will be charming, even though their outfits . . ." As if Donna's sharply lifted chin were a conductor's baton, Josie raised her voice half an octave. "The idea of the Ladle's guests making the bridesmaids' dresses was inspired. The birth of a cottage industry! Who loaned the extra sewing machines?"

"Volunteers."

"Volunteers. Without which we'd be nowhere. Did anybody visit May this week?"

The question was delivered in a quiet tone, as if between arias. In a similar everyday manner, Donna said, "I went to see her yesterday. She's still sitting up and talking. Pam will visit tomorrow."

May had been one of the first guests at Donna's Ladle, just as Josie had been one of its first volunteers. Now May was dying in the hospital.

Josie drew a breath and returned to her operatic manner. "The

Wednesday Group catering the wedding buffet—that's another original touch. Will they dish out the usual veggie melt?"

"Stop it, Josie; they're making salmon mousse." Donna's voice was low. "I know you wanted to give me a grand catered reception, but how could I refuse the Wednesday Group? Anyway, you're doing enough—all the facilitating."

"Yes, well," said Josie, looking down. "This potato is entirely black." Altogether rotted; nothing left of the original spud. Perfect, in its way. Death in a skin. She threw the potato into the barrel of discards. "As facilitator I request a rehearsal. I admire your wish to be married from Donna's Ladle itself. Where else? You are its founding mother and its CEO, so to speak. But in matters of sacrament, sentimentality doesn't guarantee simplicity. *Au contraire.*"

"Josie, Josie . . ."

"Oh, we can transform the dining room into a chapel, and we principals can huddle here in storage until the time to appear, but we're going to have to enter through the kitchen. There's an excellent chance that somebody will knock the salmon mousse to the floor. And in the dining room we have to plan where the judge is going to stand, not to mention that fiddler."

Donna smiled. The fiddler, Rafe's oldest friend, was the violinist in a famous quartet.

Josie stormed on. "You've got six attendants besides me. Three pairs: my twins, and Rafe's daughters, and your two staff members. Six strong-minded young women. They'll have to be orchestrated. And then there's Rafe's demon mother on that electric wheelchair. Shall we maintain some decorum? Or shall we just wander about until the old lady mows us down? And what about the damned goblet Rafe means to jump on? Who swallows the pieces? We require a rehearsal!"

Donna was silent.

Josie leaned forward theatrically, but when she spoke her voice was calm. "Existence is bafflement," she confessed. "But in life as in work, you might as well master the expected. Then you can tolerate the unexpected."

After a while, Donna said: "Let's have a rehearsal."

Josie savored her triumph in silence. "Also a rehearsal dinner," she said at last. "Quod erat demonstrandum."

Rafe never quoted ancient languages in conversation. But Josie, knowing that he was learned, had taken to flinging bits of Latin at him and sometimes at Donna.

Josie was wild about Rafe. Particularly she was wild about Rafe as partner to Donna. At the engagement party Rafe's mother had given a month earlier, Josie had confessed this enthusiasm to her wheel-chaired hostess. Together the two women surveyed the deep living room filled with people; meanwhile, Josie talked. "At last, a counter-vailing influence on my cousin the fanatic. What a bonkers life Donna has led: running a soup kitchen for seven years, living alone with a harpsichord as a pet. Pleading for dollars at suburban breakfasts. Dining meekly with major donors." Josie knew she had nattered enough. But she was on a roll, so she recited the rest of Donna's routine to herself: *Scrubbing the floor at five in the afternoon while tomorrow's beans bubble in one vat and turkey for the day after tomorrow boils in another* . . .

"I admire her too," the old lady was rasping.

. . . accompanying one woman to housing court and a second to detox and a third to the Department of Welfare. Josie's mind went rattling on; probably it was time for some tranquilizing champagne. Her eyes searched for the waiter with the tray, but she could see only Donna's two staff members, Beth and Pam; the elegant fiddler; the judge and his gorgeous black wife; assorted psychiatrists and scholars and other Jews; various relatives that she, Josie, shared with Donna, including

their notorious aunt, seventy-five if a day, still looking as if Zeus had just carried her off on his feathered back. Josie reminded herself to drop that classical comment within Rafe's hearing. Various odd friends of Donna's. The rector of Godolphin Unitarian and two of Godolphin's selectmen. "Tweedledum and Tweedledumber," she tried on Rafe's mother, but that redoubtable was wheeling away. Finally Josie saw Donna, in artfully draped wine jersey, fixed in her peculiar beauty, thirty-six years old, on her way toward marriage, motherhood, maturity; decline, dotage, death, and decomposition. It was then that Josie decided that the first dizzying step in the series needed practice beforehand.

The judge couldn't come to the rehearsal. He was suffering from one of his recurrent upper back spasms. His wife arrived in his stead, precisely on time, at six in the evening on this misty April Saturday. She and Josie stood alone in the Ladle's dining room, cleared of tables and not yet adorned for the wedding and thus revealed in all its plainness: custard walls and linoleum flooring of a somewhat darker hue. A piano not entirely upright leaned against the far wall.

"He's flat on the bed," reported the judge's wife. "Like a day-old corpse," she added cheerfully. "I will take instructions on his behalf. He's deliberated the wording of the service with Donna and Raphael. Common Prayer vows, I believe, with some Hebrew additionals."

Josie showed her where the judge would stand—at the end of the dining room farthest from the kitchen, near the piano. "We'll drape the piano with something. There'll be a bit of a procession. The violinist will play. He can't rehearse either; he's doing a concert in New York tonight, flying back first thing in the morning. I hope we won't have one of our famous fogs."

"Good weather," promised the judge's wife.

"Rafe's brother will wheel in their mother," Josie continued. "She doesn't use that electric contraption indoors, thank God; she's terrifying enough on an ordinary wheelchair. She'll be followed by three sets of bridesmaids, and then by me, and then by the bride and groom. They're giving themselves to each other, or giving each other away, the symbolism is wearying. Oh, Donna, Rafe, there you are," she called to the couple, who had appeared soundlessly in the rear vestibule that led from the alley. "The happy pair!" she shouted, adding to her companion in an undertone, "Show me the bride who *doesn't* want to defenestrate her groom on the eve of the wedding!" The judge's wife did not reply. "And the rest of the party, hello!" Josie called, turning toward her husband and their twins, who were clattering down the stairs from the boulevard, followed by Rafe's two daughters. "The wedding guests will enter through that door, as Stuyvesant and the girls just did," said Josie, noting that all four young women were in jeans; the rehearsal dinner had suddenly gone informal. "There'll be no ushers; Rafe says that ushers are for funerals. But there'll be a strongman. Bucky, one of the Ladle's volunteers, great old gorilla, he said he'd carry anybody who needs carrying. He's also constructing the canopy. Our aunt is floralizing—Bucky's term. They're working together, or so I'm told. And here's Pam!"

Pam had come downstairs from the church proper. "I don't trust that elevator," she said. Rafe's stocky brother followed her. The elevator near the sexton's closet, which had not worked for years, groaned within its column. It stopped creaking, it opened; out shot Rafe's mother.

Donna and Rafe approached, still silent, but Josie saw that they were not at odds. They were composed, as if they'd been married for years.

Beth blew in from the boulevard. "Sorry. I was at the hospital visiting May." She paused and flushed; many faces were turned toward hers. "May's just the same. No change."

"The wedding's at three tomorrow," Josie reminded them loudly. "We'll assemble in storage at two. Let's go there now."

She herded the group through dining room and kitchen into storage. Then she began to describe the proceedings. Her directions were immediately lost amid various murmurous exchanges. Rafe's older daughter and Donna, leaning against the refrigerator, were talking about the sick woman, May.

"She used to sell trinkets," Josie heard Donna say. "But after a while she forgot how to make change."

Beth and the twins were examining some deformed turnips. The judge's wife was talking to Stuyvesant. Rafe's younger daughter—dark, with the wide nostrils of a pretty monkey—took a paperback out of her pocket.

"When we are ready to enter," Josie said in a louder voice, and then: "Please listen to me!" A chastened silence, followed by a hiss from the steam pipes. "When we are ready to enter, I'll get the fiddler's attention, and he'll begin to play."

"The wedding march," sighed Beth. "I love the wedding march."

"The meditation from *Thaïs*," corrected Rafe.

"Dad!" Rafe's older daughter shook her headful of blond curls. "What an affected choice. And not even a march. What's the recessional—'The Flight of the Bumblebee'?"

"The usual Mendelssohn," her father told her.

Rafe's younger daughter, still reading, sat down on a sack of onions.

"The violinist will play," Josie repeated. She turned to Rafe's brother. "You will escort your mother into the dining room. Then Pam and Beth will march, then the twins, then you two," looking at Rafe's daughters. "Then me. Then Donna and Rafe. Shall we try it now? One run-through should be sufficient." She turned to the judge's wife. "Would you please go out into the dining room and stand in the place

I showed you. And Stuy, would you do the music on the piano?"

They left. From the doorway of storage the view through the kitchen to the dining room was interrupted by a wall. The eleven people in storage trustingly waited. Rafe's younger daughter turned a page. They waited some more.

"Stuy?" called Josie.

"I don't know *Thaïs*," he rumbled back.

"Play the 'Wedding March,'" yelled Rafe's older daughter.

Another silence; then came "Maple Leaf Rag." Josie nodded to Rafe's brother. He wheeled the old lady into the kitchen and disappeared. Josie nodded to Pam and Beth. They started forward. "Stately, stately," she called after them. "Ignore the piano; he's gone mad," for Stuyvesant had moved into Fats Waller. "Count slowly to ten, then start," she said to her twins. "You, too, please," she said to Rafe's daughters.

She charged into the kitchen after Pam and Beth, circled the center island of sinks and reached the doorway to the dining room ahead of them. She raced in, and stationed herself against the side wall. "Wheel the chair to the front," she called to Rafe's brother. "There'll be a space left in the first row. Then as best man you'll stand before the judge. Pretend that Mrs. Judge is Mr. Judge."

Rafe's brother did as he was told. Pam and Beth were moving forward. The twins draggled in, laughing. "Together, together!" Josie yelled. They fell into step. Rafe's daughters now entered the long room. This looked like a wedding! Of course no one was dressed for a ceremony. But tomorrow there might be trouble with costumes, too; the bridesmaids' dresses were not yet finished. And there might be a problem with properties as well. She had peeked into the sewing room earlier; the canopy and trellises that Bucky and his sons were constructing seemed to be in hundreds of pieces. Counting to ten, Josie walked back to the kitchen doorway, wheeled, and began her own advance. Stuyvesant was playing "Melancholy Baby."

She turned her head and bellowed back toward the kitchen, "Donna! Don't start yet, wait until I'm under the canopy. I'm approaching the canopy. I'm under it! Start!"

Raphael and Donna entered. They proceeded not arm and arm but hand in hand, like children in a pageant, like lovers in a garden, like a couple she knew who had walked to the funeral of their ten-year-old with their hands clasped like children in a pageant, like lovers in a garden. That couple had later divorced. Donna and Rafe would, God willing, not lose a child, not the one Donna was carrying nor any other; no one in this room should lose a child. She herself still mourned her stillbirth, Donna and Rafe would, God willing, not divorce, either, no time left for that. Donna and Rafe knew divorce was due to too much individualism, Donna and Rafe were aware that they were only mites on the planet. Fourteen years separated them. Several fifty-year-old single women in town were understandably annoyed at Rafe's choice. But such a choice was the way of the world, Josie knew, always had been, always would be. Ignore the current little sideshow of older women and younger men; you couldn't open a ladies' rag without reading about some such pair, ridiculous, a fad like the Hoola Hoop. Anatomy was fate, no matter how indignantly denied. Donna and Rafe were now halfway down the imaginary aisle, in the exact middle of the empty room. Good for Donna to have surrendered at last to Rafe's desire for a child. Donna had listened also to the ticking of her body. All too soon she would get an earful of the next biological clock, the one that ticked in men and women alike, kept in working order by a scarlet being who squatted in our entrails and held to his pointed ear the timepiece with our date of death already inscribed on its back. Donna and Rafe had reached the phantom canopy. Their arrival coincided with the final chords of some Hungarian mishmash, part Brahms, part Stuyvesant.

"Dearly beloved," said the judge's wife. "Tomorrow my husband will conduct the dignified service that you have designed. He will make a heartfelt blessing, for he has long loved you, Raphael, and he has come to love you, Donna." Her voice rang with a Caribbean joy. "After the vows and the breaking of the glass you two, wedded, will kiss"—they kissed lightly; Josie's own lips tingled—"and then the procession will reverse. And where will the receiving area be?" she asked Josie.

"Halfway down the left wall. Just outside the sewing room," said Josie, thinking with renewed dread of the mangled carpentry inside. "You'll all line up there. People will drift over to congratulate you. Meanwhile, Bucky and his gang will fold the chairs and set up the buffet table. Let's just run it through," she suggested.

To her surprise everyone complied. Stuyvesant struck up the Mendelssohn recessional. Donna and Rafe high-stepped to the rear of the room and then glided around its perimeter to the closed door of the sewing room, followed by the attendants, followed by Rafe's mother and his brother. For a moment the tableau held, all those interesting and attractive faces; she'd still remember them years from now when she was drooling in a home. Then Rafe's younger daughter broke ranks and sat down on the floor and opened her paperback and began to read.

On Sunday morning Donna awoke to the sound of church bells. Ten o'clock. She was expected at the Ladle at two. She had four hours to kill. Other people were doing all the work. Rafe was in his house playing *paterfamilias* to his ingathered children. Bucky and his sons were putting the finishing touches to some sort of canopy. The Wednesday Group was beating eggs. And Pam and Beth and Josie were correcting the bridesmaids' dresses. Apparently the A-shaped muslin gowns created by the Ladle's guests still needed work, though Beth and Pam had protected Donna from this knowledge, as they had tried to protect her from so much in recent weeks—from Roxanne's confusion, for instance; from Bitsy's arrest for shoplifting. "Am I not still a staff member?" she had demanded of their red faces after she heard from a volunteer about Bitsy. "Or am I a china doll? Pregnancy is not a disease. Marriage is not an embalming!"

The bridesmaids' dresses were a mixed lot, Rafe's younger daughter had confided at last night's rehearsal dinner. Pam's was perfect, the girl went on—it might have been tailored in Paris. Someone in that impromptu atelier knew what she was doing. Beth's fit her beautifully, too, although the couturière had forgotten the hem. Josie's twins' gowns had yellow chalk marks on the outside that wouldn't come off. "The dresses sort of look like patterns. But Josie swears that they make a frank fashion statement and may even become the rage." As for the dresses sewn for Rafe's daughters, the situation with them was nip and tuck—and at this inadvertent pun, Donna's confidante grinned, impish, irresistible. She must look just like her mother, Donna thought; how appealing her mother must have been, how much Rafe must have loved her. "... nip and tuck whether they'll be finished in time. But safety pins and Scotch tape have gotten us all through many an event. Not to worry, Donna."

Donna wasn't worrying. Not about the dresses, anyway. She worried as always about the Ladle's guests—Bitsy's intransigence, Karin's hallucinations. She wondered how long Roxanne could manage to feed and warm herself and the other squatters in that abandoned house in Dorchester. And May, dying in the hospital—would her estranged sister show up at the funeral?

And she worried about her vocation. Her vocation seemed to be slipping, gradually but unstoppably, like a patient on the terminal ward. Often she succumbed to the blandishments of ease—to long weekend mornings with Rafe and the newspaper; to their favorite steamy Hungarian restaurant whose caraway had aphrodisiac properties; to boredom, which was a kind of enchantment. One recent Thursday afternoon, after a fund-raising speech to a women's club, she had not rushed back to the Ladle as was her custom. Instead she had gotten off the trolley at a different stop and had wandered through an out-of-the-way neighborhood. Three-decker houses surrounded a children's park. Donna, on a bench next to the sandbox, watched the children, gazing for a while at a moist lower lip and then at a trusting nape. Next she turned her attention to an infant at the breast, his hand a petal on his mother's veined whiteness; had seen him hoisted gently to her shoulder, turn his mouth toward her ear, belch liquid onto her neck, while the mother merely laughed, as if the stuff were balm. The baby fell asleep. Donna kept watching. "Replete, wanting nothing further from the afternoon," she told Rafe later.

"A milky child," he agreed, his eyes warm on her face.

"Not the child. Me."

He maintained his loving gaze and withheld comment. But who needed a psychiatric interpretation with Allie around? "Fuck freedom," Allie suggested to Donna the very next day. "Babies is all."

Now Donna made coffee and sat by the window to drink it. Her dress, an ankle-length cylinder of pleats, hung on her bedroom door. Her shoes were the identical ivory. Her cotton maternity underpants were the color of a robin's egg. Her pearls had belonged to her dear dead mother, and she had borrowed a headband of creamy silk roses from her oldest friend. She was thoroughly a bride. And so she had better take a long scented bath—Rafe's bookish daughter had surprised her with a gift of bath salts—and wash her hair, and cry...

The telephone rang.

The young voice belonged to a nurse from the hospital, from the medical wing on the fourth floor, May's wing.

"She's going."

"Oh!"

"I'm sorry."

"Oh!" cried Donna again. And then, in better control, "I'll be right over."

She threw on dungarees and a sweater. She ran down the three flights to the building's basement and unlocked her bike and wheeled it up the narrow stairs. Then, unwashed hair flying, she whizzed along the warm and silent Sunday streets.

The hospital too had a Sabbath calm. Donna parked her bike in the area behind the kitchen and waved through the window to a cook she knew. He opened the back door and she went upstairs in the service elevator. A trolley of cartons kept her company.

On first sight May looked no different. On Wednesday, though very pale, she had been alert. Now, still the color of her own pillow, she lay with her eyes closed, her sparse whiskers black against the bloodless skin. The dark hair on her head was as damp as a pelt. Her mouth was slightly open. A tube snaked under the covers toward her belly—a morphine drip, Donna supposed. Tubes in her nose helped her breathe. Other equipment burbled unseen.

A nurse—one of the rare elderly ones, not the sprite who'd telephoned—was standing by the bed. Her fingertips rested on the aluminum bar.

"She's unconscious?" Donna asked.

"That she is. 'Twill not be a hard going. Are you the sister?"

"No, a friend. May I touch her?"

The nurse nodded. "Hold her poor hand. Stay by her. One of these minutes she'll just stop breathing. The button's here, beside her shoulder." She moved away from the bed, and Donna saw that she was lame.

Donna stood looking down at May while the nurse stumped away. Then she shifted her gaze to the still life on the bedside table: a glass with a bent straw, a crescent bowl, a box of Kleenex with one tissue festively erect. She pushed the table out of the way. She dragged a chair with a plastic seat close to the bed. She lowered the aluminum bar. She sat down, leaned forward, and took May's hand in her own.

How long had she known this woman—six years, seven? In the beginning May had still been peddling cheap jewelry in a Boston subway station. A customer had mentioned the basement lunchroom for women only, just across the line in Godolphin. A place that asked no questions, gave no advice, merely provided a free meal and a bathroom and sometimes a coat or a pair of shoes. May never turned down warm clothing. In all weathers she wore the dark knitted hat of a railway hobo. It concealed her hair and her mottled brow so that she presented to the world only the light blue eyes, the smile with its half-dozen discolored teeth, the whiskers, and the determination not to be separated from her friend the bottle.

"Are you sure May's a woman?" one of the volunteers had asked.

"We do get some cross-dressers," Donna responded evenly. "Have you seen Kelly in her colonel's regalia? And one of our new guests is in the process of undergoing a sex change; genitally, she's already a woman although her voice is still a problem."

"Which one is that one?" the volunteer eagerly inquired.

"She's not here today. May is female, I can assure you." May had menstruated, had fornicated, had borne children. Donna had seen her breasts in the shower—flat brownish triangles. "We haven't had men in women's clothing recently."

During the early years dragsters had sometimes pranced in. She'd always asked them politely to leave. "Darling, I protest!" one had said. "I'm writing a term paper," another had tried.

"I mean it," she'd told them. Donna the Unswerving, Rafe called her when he heard that tone.

But May, despite her tramp's clothing and her hirsutism, was a woman, their sister; and now, dying on clean sheets, she looked particularly feminine. Perhaps death did that to you: restored the charm of your gender. Or perhaps, Donna thought with a sigh, the nurses had accomplished it with sponges and soap.

May had often been grimy the last few years, despite the occasional sobering dousings under the Ladle's shower. Usually she smelled. Waking her up at three in the afternoon, when the Ladle closed, was a daunting task. She would mumble yes, yes, yes, her arm in its rumpled sweater covering her reddened eyes, her breath doggy. Then she'd fall asleep again. Donna would let her lie for a while; then a rougher shake. Finally May would stumble off to the bathroom. They'd hear her retching. "I just cleaned up in there," someone would complain, not unreasonably. Soon she'd emerge, wheedle a cup of coffee. Donna would escort her out. "If it gets too cold, come sack out at my place."

A rare invitation. May appreciated her special status. "You're a brick." But she preferred doorways, or telephone booths, or the safe triangle of a certain automatic teller, whose patrons had become used to her.

Then the stroke. The enforced hospital stay. The casual drying out that occurred there, as if May could have shrugged off the habit at any time, had anyone bothered to suggest it. "Half her brain is gone," said a young doctor to Donna. "In a way that makes everything easier."

She recognized Donna and Pam, couldn't seem to place Beth. "But you keep coming by, kid; I'll put a name to that face."

Then the discovery of disease. It had been suspected for a while, but who dared to do an exploratory on a woman in her condition? Finally they managed a bronchoscopy.

"What a transformation," said Donna to Rafe. "One month she's a derelict drinking herself to death on the curbside. The next month she's a gentlewoman succumbing to metastatic breast cancer in the hospital."

"You are what you die of," he offered.

What would he die of? she wondered. Would the manner of his dying become him? Was life with its milestones and surprises a rehearsal for death? Maybe life was a throwaway prologue and being dead was the important activity... May's eyebrows twitched, then twitched again.

All deaths recall the ones that came before. Her mother's, her father's, the ten-year-old daughter of a friend of Josie's. And Phyllis, one of the Ladle's guests, gone within a week, her skin as yellow as manila hemp. And Olive, last fall. Now May, this fierce, impudent, secretive woman. May had granted them the usual few crumbs of biography: vanished father, saintly mother, brothers early dead—one in a fire. "They dragged me in to identify him," she had told Pam. "Who could put a name to that crisp? In the end they did it by the teeth."

And a sister. For the Ladle's women there was always a sister. Sometimes she was imaginary. So much was imaginary: children, uncles, bank accounts, pilot's licenses. Sometimes she was real; only her kindnesses were invented. "My sister, the one up in Concord, she's having the biggest Thanksgiving," Roxanne had confided to Beth. "Goose and peasant. She wouldn't bother with no turkey. I have to bake a pecan pie. Do you think you could lend me some rum?"

May's sister was real. Donna knew that, because the sister had telephoned the Ladle. "May's been calling me again. Can you stop her?" said the voice, wet with sorrow. "It's all I can do to take care of myself. Miss?"

The sister had not visited May in the hospital.

May now sighed, a long wheezing noise. She forgot to inhale. Donna inhaled loudly, to remind her. May inhaled. Then she wheezed again, and was again silent. Donna inhaled. The process repeated, and repeated, and repeated. Donna kept them both going, like the dancer who leads. She imagined herself in white tie and tails, whirling her partner, bending her low, lifting her up, spinning her and catching her and beginning the routine again.

But death was winding around the exhausted pair. Donna could feel its steely web.

Church bells rang somewhere. Nurses came in, went out. Would she like some tea? someone asked very politely. Donna listened to the formalities of the change of shift. Trays clattered. Would she have some coffee? inquired another lady-in-waiting. Bells rang again.

It was two o'clock. Donna stood up. She lifted May's hand and kissed it and put it down again. She raised the bar of the bed. To push the button lying on the pillow would alarm someone without cause. Instead she went to the door and peered into the hall. A man looking for a room number avoided Donna's eyes as if she were an enchantress. Two house officers strolled past deep in conversation. A tall nurse with a bony Aztec face answered Donna's silent plea and walked quickly into the room toward the bed. "A change?"

Donna followed her. "No change. But I have to leave."

A woman appeared in the doorway. She had May's pale blue eyes and May's soft mouth. "May," said the woman, not heeding Donna, not heeding the nurse, stumbling toward the bed, leaning across the bar, lifting the hand that Donna had just laid on the blanket, pressing it to her own lips.

The nurse and Donna stood like courtiers. May's next exhalation seemed a gratified sigh. The nurse slipped behind Donna and left the room. Donna would have attended the ceremony of reunion for a minute or two longer. But she too was needed elsewhere.

She walked without haste into the corridor. Then she flew. She ran down the stairs, almost falling. "It's all right, Baby," she whispered, arm across her abdomen. She ran through the front door and raced around the side of the building. She neglected to wave to the cook. She mounted her bike and pedaled home. The answering machine was blinking itself into extinction. She would have to skip the scented bath, the shampoo, the tears; she would have to skip even a shower. She sniffed her underarm. A chivey smell, not unpleasant. She peeled off jeans, sweater, and, after a second's thought, underwear. She put on the blue panties and a lace bra and pantyhose from the drugstore; she put on the wedding outfit: dress, pearls, shoes, and headband. She checked herself in the mirror. A column of a woman, not conspicuously pregnant, needing lipstick. She applied lipstick.

It was quarter to three. Biking the four blocks to the Ladle would save a few minutes. But the dress might catch in the bike spokes. So she exchanged her shoes for sneakers, slipped on her trench coat, put the shoes in the pocket of the coat, and left the apartment.

On the way to her wedding she passed many people. Two small girls trotting home from Little League practice looked at her with interest. "It must be Purim," said one to the other. Two boys in the uniforms of a different team didn't notice her at all. An old woman said, "Lovely, dear." A nanny behind a pram sniffed. Somebody in a pickup truck honked.

She slipped into the alley behind the church. She saw an empty bottle, a rolled newspaper, three turquoise socks. The alley always became a dormitory in good weather. She resisted the urge to pick the stuff up.

She paused in the vestibule of the basement. Through one doorway she could see the kitchen and through the other the dining room. In the kitchen a group of familiar middle-aged women were skidding around with bowls and platters. An ordinary Wednesday scene, though this was Sunday. But the dining room had been transformed into a woodland theater. Hundreds of leafy garlands hung from ceiling and walls. There were rows and rows of seats on either side of an aisle. Each seat was occupied. Down the aisle a jade carpet ran toward an archway entirely covered with gardenias. Within this bower stood the judge. He wore, above his judicial robe, a large cervical collar. An embroidered yarmulke completed the outfit. He was talking to the violinist, who held his golden instrument by the throat. Their conversation seemed animated. The audience in its chairs was also animated. The Ladle's guests—about thirty had appeared, Donna estimated—had shyly seated themselves together in three rows on the right, though for some of them—Bitsy and Karin, for instance—the length of the entire dining room was sometimes insufficient to prevent squabbling. No one was squabbling now. Donna inspected the other rows. Rafe's friends. Her friends. Rafe's mother's Great Ideas Club. And other warm hearts. Bucky was wearing a pin-striped suit and could have passed for an ambassador.

The kitchen was the most direct route to storage. But Donna instead raced through the dusty passageway behind the oil burner. She arrived at the far end of storage, and, taking advantage of the fact that none of the people arguing at the other end was looking her way, she speedily kicked off sneakers and put on shoes and dropped raincoat and then stepped forward, just as Rafe turned his head. His face was white—as white as death. "I'm sorry to be late," said Donna. "My goodness, you thought something had happened to me." Rafe's flush told her that an accident was not what he had feared. She moved faster until she stood face to face with her almost husband. She grabbed his upper arm with her two hands, squeezed it in fury and love and sorrow. "You thought I was standing you up," she said. "Just *try* and lose me. I'm yours forever," she said: Donna the Unswerving.

Josie whirled. She ran through the kitchen and stood in the green paradise that had yesterday been a basement dining room. She caught the fiddler's eye. She ran back to storage, followed by the first notes of the Massenet. She motioned to Rafe's brother. He wheeled his mother into the kitchen. The Wednesday Group separated to let them pass. Next, Pam and Beth. Side by side, holding armfuls of daisies, in frocks that Yves St. Laurent would have been proud to acknowledge, they marched smiling into the kitchen and out again, beyond her control. Next, her own pretty daughters, their dresses trimmed in yellow chalk. Then Rafe's daughters, the confident blond one and the little dark one. Josie snatched the book from the hands of the dark one and replaced it with daisies. "Oh, sorry, thanks," the young woman said; what a grin. They moved past on their way into the kitchen, hold your bouquets steady, girls, and what's that pink stuff in the back of the blond's dress, at her waist. Good Lord, it's her underwear, the morning's frantic basting had come loose. Josie raced after the sisters and, just as they were about to enter the dining room, refastened the gaping skirt to its bodice with a safety pin and covered her work with masking tape, the exact color of the muslin, you'd think one had been dyed to match the other. Ran back to storage, picked up one bouquet and thrust another into Donna's hands, cold as ice they were, where *had* she been hiding this past hour? Ran through the kitchen for the last time.

Now it was she who stood in the doorway. All vows recall the ones that came before. She sought Stuyvesant's eyes among the hundreds of pairs that were turned toward her. She found him at once. They smiled at each other. She marched grandly forward, down the aisle, through the ranks of bridesmaids, and this time it was the *front* of that damned dress that had separated at the waist, pink nylon appeared at the gap, the skin beneath the shroud, the flesh beneath the skin. Too late to do anything about anything. Josie took her place under the canopy opposite Rafe's brother. And turned to watch as there emerged from the kitchen a man, flourishing and handsome, and a large-eyed woman, beautiful though in a haunted way, as if she had been summoned from coffin to nuptials like a bride in one of those ghostly tales, nauseating thought, must banish it this instant. An oath, a prayer, a toast! To them, Josie breathed. To birth and death and the mess in between; might as well call it life, everybody else does.

THE COOK

wwwwwwwwwwwwwwwwwwwww

Tuesday

On these heavy afternoons the children squabble. Pavel and I let them argue, even slap; but if they bite or scratch we separate them. No trouble; they cower at once.

At present there are six in our care. This morning, when not at each other's throats, they managed to turn the dusty courtyard of this old mountainside hacienda into a theater. They shot one another from behind posts. Then they staged a royal pageant. Maria and Jacopo—who in real life are surely sister and brother, probably twins—were married beside the dry fountain. I crouched on the stones, watching. The smallest boy stood beside me, his warm fingers smoothing my red beard. The two other small boys enacted the honor guard, wearing soldiers' hats folded from newspapers. Maria and Jacopo wore two of my saucepans for crowns—their coronation had preceded their wedding in a thrifty blend of ceremonies.

Ana played the priest. She is the thinnest of the children, having most recently arrived. In an old black raincoat left behind by a fourteen-year-old when he was transferred, she looked more or less clerical.

"I can't finish!" she cried in the middle of the proceedings.

Jacopo, already kneeling, brought his fist down on her bare foot.

"What's wrong?" I called.

"I have no prayer book!" screamed Ana.

I gave her my loose-leaf collection of pastry recipes. The wedding party re-formed. Ana held the book open at her waist. The black raincoat hung to her ankles. She is undergrown for twelve—not much taller than I, and I am a dwarf. A flat black hat, which may once really have been the hat of a priest, shaded her bony, ugly, old-woman's face. In a pious voice she imitated the shallow sincerity of the vanished padres. She reminded me of the mild little fellow who paid us a visit last year. In fact he was on the run, though he never said so. Our final view of him was from the rear, as he was being carried away by a mercenary with tough buttocks. The soldier was able to hold the unprotesting man of God under one arm. Like a pumpernickel, Pavel remarked.

After the royal wedding, Ana, still in coat and hat, helped me boil beans. She is currently our oldest child. Almost at the menarche. Of course she is not diseased—we are not given sick kids to tend. But it will take me months, perhaps a year, to bring her to anything like robustness. She is as spindly as a McDonald's french-fried potato—yellow, bent, almost without shoulders.

Saint McDonald's, the youngsters call the place. The arches seem churchly, I suppose. Much of the kids' food before they came here originated in Saint McDonald's—scraps discovered in the alley, or begged from patrons hurrying out with a bag, or wrenched from a feeble hand. There are three McDonald's in the city—one near the cathedral, one on the edge of the park, and one downtown. The downtown McDonald's is the favorite of abandoned children. The kids collect on the deep ledges of the curved windows and crane their necks to get a glimpse of the ceremony of eating. There are two or three children on every ledge at any time. On rainy afternoons the two or three multiply quickly. Four, six, eight; and then little ones find a place on the laps of older girls, or on the backs of older boys. Children sitting on the sidewalk lean against the shins of those sitting on the brick ledge. Some bold boys secure a single foothold on the ledge and hold themselves upright with their fingertips on the window, as if by a heavenly suction. The whole wet, ragged, fierce-eyed crew looks as if it is witness to a miracle. Buns and fish sticks.

Wednesday

This morning our slow-witted servant said that *we* are the miracle. She tramps down the mountain once a week to scrub our floors and wash our clothing and beat the single rug. Today as always she touched my hump for luck, and she smiled shyly at Pavel's face—such a thin, intelligent face. In any line-up you would pick out Pavel as the former graduate student in philosophy. Neo-Platonic ecstasy was his special field. "Salvador," said the servant.

Pavel said only, "Gracias." But tonight he expanded on her premise. We *have* rescued the children, he told me. The major's patrol—barrel-shaped men: Big Bellies, we call them—do the preliminary work, crashing into the cellar dugouts or the sewer squats, choosing this boy or that girl. But we are the heart of the process.

"Stomach," I modified. I like to call organs by their rightful names.

He waved an impatient hand. "We rescue them from prostitution and snuff films. From cholera and typhoid. From starvation. We convert them to a rude health. We give them time."

I said nothing. The children were sleeping upstairs, recklessly using up their time. The hacienda was dark except for the single bulb swaying from the ceiling in my kitchen as if it had been hanged.

Thursday

I weeded the little garden today. We grow cabbages and sweet squash and peas and yams. Our belled cow grazes on the far side of a wire fence.

Then I drove the pickup truck to the market just east of the city. The farmers hailed me by my nickname, "Chicago"—I grew up there, before drifting south and further south. They offered cigarettes. Their shrewd women ignored me. They know that I shun the carcasses of goats, on which flies are always feasting. They know we keep our own chickens. So they screamed their prices not at me but at restaurant chefs and embassy cooks.

I did inspect fish on planks—white perch spotted with red, silvery trout. A fisherman's little boy rapidly enumerated their virtues. Eventually he offered me his aunt.

I admired the fish. But mostly our diet is vegetarian. So I bought only corn and beans, the staples of the country. Corn and beans used to be damned as lacking in nutritional value. Now they are recognized as an enriched diet, and wealthy New Yorkers, I'm told, serve each other polenta and black bean soup—exactly the breakfast I turn out for my children, seasoned with chilis and garnished with orange slices and boiled greens.

Friday

Jacopo and I slaughtered three chickens. I've taught the kids how to wring the neck with one quick twist. I've taught them how to pluck the feathers, drain the blood, remove the organs, and bake the birds in a clay pot (our chickens are too stringy to roast). This morning Maria stewed the gizzards and kidneys and hearts. Ana fried the livers.

Tonight we dined at the carved table in the big room. On weekends the major doesn't send for Pavel. The Big Bellies don't come. New children are not delivered. Current children are not transferred. We have two days without visitors, without disturbance—two days and three nights. Pavel and I sat opposite each other. Candles illuminated the faces of the children—some wizened, some already plump—and left in shadows the cupboard with its broken door and the old lace curtains.

Sunday

The rains have not yet begun. Flowers erupt on the edge of the forest. Yesterday and again today we walked along the trail to the forest stream. In the water I resemble a dolphin, Pavel said, with my slick hump. I laughed: A dolphin with a red beard? Last night and tonight, in my room, I told the children tales remembered from my childhood. I spoke in Spanish, though I first heard the stories in English, and they were originally told in German or Norwegian. A gallimaufry of tongues. The tongue too is an organ, though not transplantable—not yet, anyway. I sat on the sagging velvet couch, with Maria beside me, and Jacopo beside her. Ana occupied a low stool. The little boys lay on the floor. One sucked his thumb. The second rested his head on the third.

"You're hurting my stomach," the underneath one complained.

"Abdomen," I corrected.

"Abdomen." His cheeks were slightly fuller than they were last week, I noticed.

The fullness is my doing—the result of my attention and my expertise. Though I knew physiology when I was recruited for this job, I was ignorant of the rules of nutrition. I educated myself in cookery just as I once trained myself for the stage and also for the classroom, just as I taught myself Spanish when I first came to this country. Texts about the chemical properties of sweetness and the cultural determinants of diet line my bedroom walls. The children ignore them. They want only fables, fables not read from a book but remembered, like gossip. They want reports of transformations, of elevations from peasantry to aristocracy. Children are such snobs. They want to hear about a small band of chums outwitting an ogre. They want news of elves who assist a poor shoemaker. Like a good parent I give them what they crave—the stories—and also what they need. Milk. Greens. Fruit. Whole grains, which are not easy to come by here. But I come by them. I bake bread frequently.

Monday

I felt dull all day. The weekend skittered by like a child running from a thug.

Tonight I baked bread. Maria and Jacopo joined me in the kitchen. Pavel was out. The black car had strained up the mountainside to fetch him. Sitting in the backseat like an ambassador he was transported to the major. He will be returned shortly before dawn, charged with philosophical enlightenment. He will have new tobacco for his pipe. He will have a new insight into utilitarianism. And in a few days some emaciated but clean children will be chauffeured to our hacienda, fresh from the nurse and doctor. The nurse will have washed and deloused them. The doctor will have pronounced them free from illness and without inner malformity. That is: their hearts, lungs, livers, and kidneys are normal and—assuming a continued regime of my good food and of Pavel's attentive guardianship—will become encased in well-fed, hygienically functioning bodies.

But these new children have not yet arrived to be fattened. Nor have any of our current children been transferred, though one of the little boys asleep upstairs, the one who learned to distinguish abdomen from stomach, has grown so sturdy that I suspect he will not be with us much longer. I can imagine him escorted into a scrubbed alabaster room with gleaming equipment. In a similar room on the other side of the tiled wall lies, say, the daughter of a planter, a lovely girl afflicted with diseased kidneys, or an enlarged heart. She dozes, her golden hair loose on the pillow. Does my boy feel the presence of the sleeping princess whose life will be saved by a peasant lad? Probably not; he is too excited by the figures gowned in green who await him. He hails them as if they were old friends—shoemakers' elves, grown magically tall.

I do not know that this will happen—the encounter of the child with elves who are not really elves. If I *knew* that my youngsters met deception and discomfort after their transfer, I would bundle the six we have now into a sack, put the sack into the pickup truck, and drive pell-mell to the border, where we would all be shot.

One of the other little boys is also growing rosy.

I do not sleep much. Maria and Jacopo also do not sleep much. They remain thin and sallow, as if they are not receiving the full benefit of my nutrition. Ana too fails to thrive. Pavel thinks she might be bulimic.

At midnight the twins were still sitting at the kitchen table, handsome despite their skinniness. Since their coronation last Tuesday next to the dry fountain, they have adopted the sly winking manner of kings' courtiers. But, though clever mimics, they are not nobility. They are the children of the impoverished, the demented, the wicked, the helpless, or the disappeared—how else could they have been found ragged and smelly and starving in the window of Saint McDonald's?

When my dough had risen, I took the towel off the pan and bent toward the oven. I crouched there, unmoving, thinking of the little boys upstairs, fists curled under their chins. I knew how I must look from the rear, with my hump higher than my head—a small figure, never much taller than a child, at that moment even shorter than a child, shorter than Maria, shorter than Jacopo. I felt as unresisting as that priest who was carried so easily away. But Maria and Jacopo failed to notice that they could have tumbled me into the oven without effort, could have slammed the door on my exhausted silence. They are not so clever after all, our king and queen. So I must go on cooking.

THE HEADWAITER'S SON

~~~~~~~~~~~~~~~~~~~~~~~~~~~~~~~

His father (he told her) epitomized their miserable country.

What did he mean? (she inquired).

What *did* he mean . . . They were sitting on damp sand underneath the boardwalk. He scratched his left shoulder blade and then his right against a wooden post. "My father is a hotel waiter," he began. "Not an ordinary waiter, a headwaiter. At the Hotel Grande."

She nodded, her chin on her knees, her arms wrapped around her calves. Her striped skirt looked like a circus tent. How old was she, he wondered—forty-five? New England roughened women early, he'd observed.

"Your eyes are twinkling," he said, and in response to the flattery they did twinkle. "Probably you're thinking of the truly grand hotels of Europe, or of some funny servant in an operetta."

"I'm not thinking of anything," she said.

"My father's boyhood was hard." He told her of grade school fit in between seasons in the fields. He'd had some high school, too, during the time of the Coffee Government, when universal public education was first attempted. He'd worked as a busboy at the famed Rojo, destroyed in the uprising. There he became fluent in English and picked up a bit of German. He was always trusted by his employers. "My father is tall, you see. In my country to be short is to be unreliable." His own legs in their hospital whites stretched out before him on the Massachusetts sand: long, long legs. The laces on his sneakers were black.

"I do see. A tall headwaiter. But . . . an epitome, a symbol?"

He kneaded the sand with slender, capable fingers. "My father has a talent for accommodation. He has outlasted six regimes, just like the Hotel Grande—seven, if you count the Solid Front, which crumbled after a few weeks. My father is like the giant beetle who they say lives beneath the place where three rivers meet. No wars, no famines, no celebrations, no victories disturb this bug. He feeds on whichever nations other nations bury. My father's frock coat resembles a beetle's wings. In the past decade he's learned a little Russian and has picked up some words of Japanese. I myself, though better educated—I trained as a radiologist, my brothers both became architects—speak only Spanish and English."

"Your English is awfully elegant, though."

He gave her a smile, enjoying its effect. He had noticed her noticing his faun's black curls. "I read essays continually. When I am not examining X-ray plates, I am reading." He was in fact employed as a technician, not yet as a doctor; and he did read whenever there were no patients to guide to the crosshatched gray wall where they stood for their pictures. Sometimes he kept on reading even when he could see a patient waiting humbly in the corridor, knees protruding from the striped johnny . . .

"Your father wears a frock coat?" she was saying.

"He could pass for a prime minister. The atmosphere at the hotel is thoroughly imperial. The place was built in the early nineteenth century by an hidalgo aping the British. Another Spanish rogue!" He turned onto his stomach and took her poorly manicured hand in his own. "The mansion served for a while as a governor's residence. Then it became the headquarters for the revolution. After the generals' coup it turned into a private dining and drinking and you-know-whatting club for the wealthy. Just before World War II new owners made it into a real hotel, open to the public, no whores, just the ordinary bedrooms and dining facilities and a lobby with, of course, a parrot."

He grew silent. The Grande's front windows looked out on a small, dense park. He had sometimes played there as a child, under the statue of Saint Francis. Along the side street stood gloomy stone buildings behind iron fences. Splendid homes once, they now housed feeble institutions: a boarding school for the daughters of the second tier; an apartment house for pensioners; a lecture hall where a few people assembled once a week to watch art films.

The rooms at the Grande were never all taken. A *National Geographic* photographer might be staying there, or a few environmentalists on their way to the jungle. Each year the director of a college summer program brought his wife for a week. They enjoyed the out-of-the-way neighborhood while the students got immersed in Spanish at the scarred university across town. Then all went off to dig latrines and vaccinate dogs in the villages. A prize-winning Brazilian writer holed up at the Grande whenever he contemplated a bender. But he was the only famous guest. Journalists and television people and human rights dignitaries and state department officials patronized the high-rise hotels downtown, whose windows deflected sunlight onto the shacks of the wretched.

Some of this the headwaiter's son told the woman as he was kissing her palms.

"The Grande's restaurant—who comes there?" she wondered.

"Widows of judges. Retired professors. An old poet or two." And families visiting their daughters at the nearby school. And a few thin, untalkative old people from the German colony. But the private dining suites were rarely rented. Occasionally some timid girl would endure her seventeenth birthday in one of them. Sometimes a devil-may-care old lady would celebrate her eightieth.

But every so often a suite was used for an off-the-record meeting. Then his father's trustworthiness shone. Wearing the shabby frock coat, speaking some words of several languages, he could be counted on to greet each arrival with deference but never to use a name. He would scrupulously fail to recognize the American in the lemon suit, the Mexican in fatigues, the Irishman whose holster bulged under his shirt, the woman with the birthmark whom half the populace called a saint. Behind papery lids, under feathery eyebrows, the tall headwaiter betrayed no curiosity. He knew how to wheel in the dinner, how to pour wine, how to listen.

This woman under the boardwalk also knew how to listen. Her hands, thoroughly kissed, were now clasped behind her head. The gaping sleeves of her pink blouse revealed curly brown armpits. He was aroused by this sight, as he had been aroused by the first sight of her an hour ago, sitting in the doughnut shop, her head bent like a schoolgirl's over the menu. It turned out that they had come to the cheap seaside town on the same early train. Both had hoped to spend this June Thursday swimming. But there was too much wind; warning signs were posted; the lifeguards had been given the day off.

She was a newscaster, she'd told him. Of course he knew she was lying. He'd seen female newscasters—their padded jackets, their gold earrings, their frosty smiles. Even properly dressed and made up she'd never resemble them—not with those wide hips, that graying hair scraped back from the temples, the glasses. He didn't mind that she was lying; she must have reasons.

He put his head in her lap. "You have an ecstatic chin," he told her.

In bed she mentioned a divorce, whispered about a daughter away at camp. Their room at the Sea View Motel had a back porch and a plug-in coffee pot. Afterwards, she made coffee while he went to the boardwalk to buy fried clams and more doughnuts. They consumed the feast on the back porch from which they could indeed view the sea, just over the dune—a sea as gray as the woman's calm eyes.

They took the train back to the city. He bought newspapers; they read of famine in Africa, war in Eastern Europe, a car bomb in Central America. They parted under the old-fashioned lamps at the public garden. He would walk southward to his basement apartment near the hospital. She would hurtle north by subway; she was expected somewhere. He did not ask for her address. A particular jungle leaf, if chewed, had an effect like hers: the chewer became loquacious, overfriendly, indifferent to consequences. Frequent chewing dulled ambition. The son of a nobody could not allow his efforts to slacken. Besides, she was too old for him. But he foresaw that her low, liquid, questioning voice would be hard to forget. He would hear it for a long time in his head.

And he was hearing it now, just two hours later, that voice, her voice, again, swimming from the bedside table. He had flipped on the radio before bending straight-kneed to untie his laces. He stayed in a clown's position, nose to kneecap, while she read the news, alertly, noncommittally, like a neighbor relaying the degradation of another neighbor. She mentioned the African famine. She gave details of the European war. She described the bombing of the car in Central America, and she devoted a few sentences to the possible perpetrators of that crime.

There was a brief, end-of-paragraph silence. He fingered one of his shoelaces. In the nation contiguous to the car-bombing one, she began; and he straightened up. She named his country.

He sat down abruptly on the bed, sneakers still tied. In that country all had been quiet for the past several months. Her voice adopted a more personal tone. He imagined her sitting at a table with a microphone, alone in a soundproofed room; behind a glass window the engineer picked at a scab on his elbow. She was still wearing the pink blouse and the striped skirt. As she laced her hands atop her head, her eyes continued to scan the notes on the table before her, notes which she must have scribbled like crazy on the subway, or perhaps in the motel room when he was out buying clams. Her hands on her head duplicated the pose of collaborators about to be shot. "Inflation has been sharply reduced. Gunfire in the hills is heard only seldom. Human rights groups report no atrocities." Her voice changed yet again, settling into an intimate monologue.

"An uneventfulness has come to the once violent country. Perhaps tomorrow will resemble today. This modest hope can be seen in the reopening of the opposition newspaper; and in the nightly reappearance, on the plaza, of a three-piece band; and in the slightly increased custom in the country's longest-running hotel, a shabby, stately place called the Grande."

She went on . . . Built early in the nineteenth century, this stone building has a spacious lobby tiled in white and black. (Had he told her that?) Overhead, a glossy brown fan stirs the tepid air. (He *had* told her that. He grinned, snapping the fingers on his right hand.) The dining room looks out on a leafy street. (Snap.) The chairs in the dining room have seats of embossed leather. (She had invented the furniture. He raised his hand soundlessly, withholding the snap.)

The Grande has survived seven regimes. (Snap.) It is tempting to interpret this history as wearily opportunistic, epitomizing the knowing helplessness of the country at large. Indeed, the dining room's headwaiter has the air of someone who has seen everything and can report nothing. (Snap.) His almost invisible limp (What limp?) hints of a beating he received (Maybe his father did favor the right leg, but only sometimes) from a goon squad he will not name (An imperfectly healed sprain; he remembered now. The old man had tripped on the way to the wine cellar a few years ago).

The austere elderly retainer continues to perform the duties he has performed for decades. He has educated his sons and buried his wife, and he owns a small pale house among other small pale houses in an area off the road to the airport. (No snap. He had stopped snapping anyway, thinking of the limp, and of his father's tale of tripping; his hands lay splayed on his thighs.) But this respectability does not seem to be the point of the waiter's ardent busyness. What *is* the point? his hot-headed and sometimes contemptuous countrymen might ask. The point is . . . (Pause. She must be leaning forward now in that greedy way of hers, as if the next nugget of thought might be the one with the gold) . . . the point is the work at hand. Whatever the slight to some sonorous ideal like democracy or green space or chastity, the task of each day must be attentively done. That is the headwaiter's message; his country, sobering up after its spree of wars and bloody truces, is perhaps listening.

For "Last Word" and its sponsors, this is Selene Haganalapougis . . . (or something; like a sullen servant he didn't even try to catch it, a long un-Latin name trailing into scanty syllables).

TO REACH THIS SEASON

~~~~~~~~~~~~~~~~~~~~~~~~~~~~

He was the last Jew in a cursed land.

A ruined country, a country of tricksters. Rich haciendas hid within the folds of mountains. Guns lay under crates of bananas. Even the green parrots practiced deception. They rested in trees, not making a sound; suddenly they rose as one, appearing and departing at the same time, leaving the observer abandoned.

The only Jew!

In truth, there was a second Jew: his son, Lex. They faced each other across the kitchen table. Lex seemed to pity the plight of his father: that on the eve of Yom Kippur there was no corner in the city where a Jew could pray for forgiveness with nine others.

"They all fled to Miami after the revolution," Lex said. "Taking their money with them."

Robert winced.

Lex said, "We'll find you a minyan, Bob." He looked at his father with compassion.

But was it really compassion? Or was it the practiced understanding of a professional social worker? Just as he had adjusted to his son's use of his first name, Robert had reconciled himself to Lex's womanish vocation. But he had not become accustomed to the nods, the murmured assents. He himself was an investment counselor.

"We've gone through the guidebooks," Lex reviewed. "Shall we hunt down a Shapiro in the telephone book? A Katz?"

Father and son laughed. Their name was Katz.

The little boy looked from one to the other.

He was a thin child despite a seemingly insatiable appetite. His name, Jaime, printed in Lex's hand, adorned the crayoned scribbles taped to the refrigerator.

There they sat, in front of those unambitious efforts, in the scarred kitchen of a small house on a muddy street in the capital city of a Jewless country. Robert was still wearing his pajamas. Far away in Beverly Hills, the drawings of Robert's granddaughter, Lex's niece, also decorated a refrigerator. Maureen Mulloy, the signature read. Maureen Mulloy printed her washerwoman's name herself. The Mulloys' Mexican housekeeper hung up the artwork. Who else could do it?—Maureen's parents practiced law twelve hours a day.

Jaime. It was pronounced Hymie. Robert speared a slice of papaya from the breakfast platter.

Lex was reading the telephone book. "No Shapiros, Bob. No Katzes, either. I'm not even listed—my phone belongs to the organization."

Robert ate a slice of pineapple.

"I'm going to call the embassy," said Lex.

"Ex," said Jaime, slapping Lex's arm. "Tengo hambre."

"Qué quiero?" Robert attempted. "I mean, *qué quieres* . . ." Lex had already risen. He and Jaime stood side by side, composedly surveying the contents of the refrigerator, a slight young man and a very slight child. "Qué quieres," Robert repeated, softly. His hesitant spoken Spanish was getting him nowhere with the boy. Why had he spent a month listening to those damned language tapes? Why had he come here, anyway?

Five days ago he had descended the aluminum steps of the airliner and stepped onto the tarmac, already blistering at two in the afternoon. He was used to hokey airports. He wasn't used to the absence of jet lag, though—he seldom journeyed from north to south. The sun had stood still on his behalf. No need to nap, no need even to eat, though on the ride from the airport Jaime had insisted on stopping for a tamale. "Ex, Ex!" he shouted, pointing to the stall. Lex pulled over. Robert smiled at Lex, indulgent parent communing with indulgent parent. But Lex ignored the smile. His attentiveness toward this soon-to-be-adopted son was meant to be approved, not joined.

The boy dropped consonants, confusing Robert. That first afternoon Robert looked at a picture book with him. *Vaca,* cow, became *aca; caballo,* horse, *callo.* Little Maureen would become Een, he supposed, if the cousins—could he really call them that?—ever met. They might not meet for a long time. The family was scattered: Robert and Betsy in Massachusetts, their daughter Mulloy née Katz out in California, Lex here in Central America, two years already, God knew how much longer.

"I'll stay until the adoption is final," Lex said late that night, after Jaime had finally gone to bed. "That's another six months. Afterwards..." He shrugged his thin shoulders. "I won't go to Chicago, that's for sure. I don't want to be in the same city as Ron." Ron was his ex-lover. "Perhaps Jaime and I will come back to Boston."

Robert nodded. "There's a bilingual program in the schools."

"Spare us." Lex rolled his eyes. "We'll continue to talk Spanish at home," he went on. "Jaime will pick up English at school, in playgrounds—as immigrant children have done for generations."

He can hardly speak his own language, Robert didn't say. *He can't count. He doesn't know colors.* "How old is he? Seven, you wrote? He's ... small."

"We use the evidence of bones and teeth," said Lex. "Central Americans are smaller than North Americans, and those with a lot of Indian blood, like Jaime, are the shortest. I'll invent a birth date when I apply for his passport. I'm going to say he's five. He's about three emotionally—a deprived three. No one ever sent him to school. When I first met him at the local orphanage a year ago he didn't talk at all. He's matured considerably since being with me."

Robert felt weary, as if jet lag had claimed him after all.

And so he went to bed, in the narrow room off the kitchen. His window faced an inner courtyard just big enough for a clothesline, a sink, and a single tree that bore hard citrus fruits. There the parrots hid.

For the next days Robert was on his own. Lex was working, and Jaime attended day-care. Robert awoke each morning to the sounds of the two at their breakfast. He figured out most of what they were saying. Jaime repeated the breakfast menu, the few chores, the routine of the day-care center. Then he repeated them again, and again. Between repetitions Robert heard the rustle of the newspaper and the slur of rubber wheels along a linoleum floor. Jaime was playing with his small toy car. He supplied the motor with his own throat. "Oom!" Twenty-five years earlier, Robert and Betsy had shared the *Globe* while, at their feet, two charming toddlers rummaged in a pile of Legos. Jaime wasn't ready for Legos, Lex had explained. He wasn't ready even for the starter set Robert had brought as a gift. Jaime didn't get the idea of construction. He had probably never seen toys before the orphanage found him—maybe he'd played with a couple of spoons, or filled an old shoe with dirt. Maureen Mulloy, Robert remembered with satisfaction and guilt, could already erect elaborate towers.

Before leaving for work Lex always knocked on Robert's half-open door.

"Entra!" Robert practiced.

Lex would then say something about the day ahead. Would Robert like to visit the university? Lex could give him a library pass. If he wandered into the outdoor market, would he please pick up a pineapple? Jaime, still on the floor with his murmuring car, poked his head between Lex's knees and then raised it, his little golden face between the denim legs solemn, or perhaps only uncomprehending.

When they were gone Robert heaved himself out of bed. He boiled bottled water for tea and ate three plain crackers. Despite this abstemious caution he invariably passed several loose stools and a quantity of brownish water. "Nothing to worry about as long as there's no blood," Lex had told him after the first episode on the second night of the stay. Lex's voice had been reassuring but his lips were prissy; and Robert, standing outside the bathroom with his belt unbuckled, raised a defiant chin like a child who had soiled his pants.

But the morning diarrhea always left him feeling better, as if he had explosively asserted himself in these austere surroundings. He next read the front page of the newspaper, using the dictionary often. Then he took a shower in cold water and shaved in cold water and got dressed. He stuffed his fanny pack with map, dictionary, currency, and flask. He wore it frontwards: a tummy pack. He put on sunglasses and a canvas cap. He left the house.

He had arrived on Saturday; by the end of yesterday, Wednesday, he had tramped all over the city. He had wandered into the barrios. He had refused Chiclets and Valium peddled by street vendors. He had stumbled upon a small archeological museum tended by some devoted women. There he learned that the great-beaked bird quetzal, known to him from a trip to Mexico, had been deified here, too.

And he stared at the windowless edifice within which members of the National Assembly, according to the new popular insult, farted their disagreements. He traveled by bus to two hot, dusty towns. Both towns had Museums of Martyrs. Back in the capital, he spent late Wednesday afternoon at the huge outdoor market. Pickpockets roamed the place, he had heard. He kept his fingers lightly on his canvas pack.

He bought Betsy a necklace of black coral. Though he loved and admired her, he missed her very little. Her absence this trip had not been a matter of dissension—*they* had farted no disagreements. There were reasons for her not coming: Lex himself had been home recently; his house here had only a single guest bed; and this not altogether regular situation—a young man becoming a father to a young boy— seemed to demand the presence of an unaccompanied older man, *the* older man, the grandfather.

Grandfather! To a child whose whole being seemed at odds with itself—the eyes soft, even tender; the mouth with its widely spaced teeth slack; the body taut, subject to occasional spasms. Yet he would become part of the family, become a Katz. Jaime Katz. What would Robert's grandfather, a rather sallow person himself, have made of such a development? He recalled Zayde Chaim shawled in silk on the Days of Awe . . . and it was at that moment, standing in the market, his hand on his canvas belly, that he remembered what day it was. The day before the day before Yom Kippur. In twenty-six hours, Kol Nidre would be sung.

Now, on Thursday morning, the embassy answered Lex's inquiry: to its knowledge there was no community of Jews in the city, in the country. Lex hung up. "They have one Jewish staff member. She goes home to Texas for the holidays."

"We've struck out."

"I'm sorry, Bob." Lex stood up. "I have to go to work. About tonight . . . I had forgotten Yom Kippur . . . a few people from the organization are supposed to come for dinner."

"Let them come," said Robert. "I'm not such a worshiper, you know. I don't fast. At your bar mitzvah I had to retool my Hebrew, and even then it wasn't so hot . . ."

"Jaime?" Lex called into the bedroom. "Rápido, por favor." He turned again to his father. "You worked over those syllables like a diamond cutter. Betsy used the transliteration . . ."

"She'd never studied Hebrew."

". . . but you were heroic. For my sake." He bowed his head.

"I wish I could do it again with my high school Spanish," said Robert, hot with embarrassment.

Lex raised his head. "For his sake," indicating with a faggy lift of one shoulder the child in the bedroom. A vat of lava bubbled in Robert's intestines; he managed to contain it. How reckless he'd been to eat that fruit. Jaime was taking his sweet time putting on his backpack. The shabbiest barrio kid in this mess of a country had a backpack. "Vámonos!" said Lex at last.

Jaime came running. Lex went outside to warm up the Jeep. Jaime turned in the doorway and waved a silent good-bye to Robert—he had yet to call him by name. Farewell here was signified by a beckoning gesture. The motion startled Robert every time; it startled him now; he took a step forward as if the child were really summoning him. Then he halted, hissing. This place! And an invitation to come closer was made in an equally ass-backwards manner: wrist limp, you wagged the back of your hand at the person you wanted, as if shaking him off.

Was the child laughing at him? No, it was only one of those wet smiles. Robert dutifully mimicked Jaime's come-hither movement. He felt like a cop directing traffic. He felt like a dirty old man. Jaime grinned and banged out. Robert bolted for the bathroom.

So he spent Yom Kippur Eve with a gaggle of gentiles. They weren't bad, Lex's fellow workers. A high-minded couple in their sixties, slack of belly, gray of hair, giving their final years to just causes. A pretty young nurse. A second, older nurse, freckled and tough. Some others. They ate rice and beans, expertly seasoned by Lex. Jaime played on the floor. Occasionally he whined for Lex's attention. Lex would finish what he'd been saying, then he'd turn his eyes to the boy and listen to the high voice repeating short, insistent phrases, and reply with a "sí" or a "no" or some grave explanation.

The adults talked of the torments of the country, the centuries of cruelty as one generation mistreated the next. "The church has a lot to answer for," said a fierce Canadian woman. "Those first missionary schools—they taught us how to inflict pain." He wondered what she meant by "us"; then he remembered that she was a Native American, a member of an indigenous people. He had met her earlier in the week when she'd dropped by. With her untidy hair and glasses and dissatisfied mouth she'd reminded him of his cousin from the Bronx. He'd met the churchy couple earlier also, at an evening lecture on cooperatives that Lex had taken him to. But this was the first social gathering Robert had attended, and he realized belatedly, when it was almost over, that it was a party in his honor.

Early the next morning they packed up the Jeep. They were to spend the weekend visiting orphanages in the mountains—Robert, Lex, Jaime, and Janet—the freckled nurse, not the pretty one.

Janet did the driving. She knew how to handle a Jeep. She drove fast on the two-lane highway, passing whenever she could. When they were stopped by a pair of very young men in fatigues, each holding a tommy gun, she answered their questions with such authority that Robert expected the teenage soldiers to stick out their tongues for her inspection. Instead they waved the Jeep on. Robert jounced along in the front seat. In the back Lex showed Jaime how the big bricks of

Legos fit together. Jaime watched indifferently, his fingers around his toy car.

They stopped late in the morning in a lush little town. There were coffee estates nearby, Janet said. In the courtyard of a restaurant, parrots watched from fronds. Jaime ran toward a cat he knew and settled down in a corner of the courtyard. The proprietress-cook brought the child a dish of pasta before welcoming the others in perfect English. She had a large, curved nose and a wide smile. "She's Chilean," Janet said when the woman had returned to the kitchen. "Her corn lasagna is terrific. She's been active in revolutionary politics." Robert understood: arms smuggling.

Two graceful waiters with angelic faces served them. Robert knew not to take their androgyny seriously. "Girlish on the outside, tough guys within," Lex had said about similar men. "Not gay." Robert did not ask whether Lex had enjoyed a native lover. Some years ago he had ascertained that his son practiced safe sex; he and Betsy wanted to know nothing further.

The corn lasagna was indeed delicious. Jaime shared his pasta with the cat. Robert would have liked to linger over coffee, to walk around this town and visit *its* Museum of Martyrs; to return at the cocktail hour and enjoy an aperitif with the South American adventuress while the parrots dozed and the waiters raped their women. Instead he paid the bill and shook her hand and bid good-bye to the birds with the proper summoning gesture.

In an hour they had left the highway and were climbing. Farms gave way to trees, boulders, scrub. Janet expertly circled craters in the road. Bracing himself against the plunges of the Jeep made Robert weary—or perhaps it was the lunchtime glass of Chilean wine. He leaned against the headrest, closed his eyes . . . and was awakened by something creeping along the side of his neck. He slapped the creature. It was a small hand.

"Sorry, Jaime. *Excúlpame.* Hey!" for the child had slapped him back.

"Jaime." Lex's voice was as authoritative as Janet's. Some low, rapid Spanish followed. Then came a tap on the shoulder and a presentation across that shoulder, in front of his face, of three Lego bricks imperfectly joined.

"Asa," said Jaime.

Casa. House. "Bueno," said Robert, mustering enthusiasm. He turned to meet those attractive eyes, that odd mouth. Lex smiled primly.

Just before two they reached the town where they were to spend the night. Robert carefully got out.

"You need a back rub," noticed Janet.

The town square was a bare knoll. A church faced the square. Its stucco walls seemed to be unraveling. The one-story inn sagged toward its own courtyard. Robert was shown to a rear bedroom. From his window he could see oxen.

Janet and Lex invited him to walk to the orphanage with them. "Thanks, no," he said. "I'll sit in the courtyard and read." And write another postcard to little Maureen.

But as soon as they had tramped off, he felt forlorn. He would not stay; he would follow his son.

They had told him that the orphanage lay two miles out of town, on the straight road west. He walked fast, at first; and within five minutes he had caught sight of them, and soon he was passing the low stone huts that they had just passed, each with its open door revealing a single room, the same room—a couple of cane rockers, a table. The same expressionless woman stood in each doorway. Children played in the mud. Had Jaime been born in such a home? More likely he had sprung from a shack like those Robert was passing now—tin and slats, the latrine in back made decent by a curtain.

Lex and Janet walked together in the middle of the road. Jaime darted from one side to the other. Janet was taller than Lex. Her light brown hair humped over her backpack and draggled down, khaki on khaki.

At the end of the road a crowd of small boys waited behind a gate. The gate was just a couple of horizontal logs, a not entirely successful attempt to keep out nearby animals. Jaime scrambled between the logs. Lex and Janet vaulted them.

Robert climbed over the top log, his bones creaking. He heard, as if in the distance, the sound of crying. Perhaps it was his own old-man's wail.

He had landed amid the boys. Boys, boys everywhere. Boys: grimy triangular faces under black bangs. Boys: wearing clothing that a decade ago and a continent away had been high style—rugby shirts, jams. Boys: none seeming above ten years old, though he knew better. Perhaps some were twelve. Boys: waiting for guns and cholera.

"Bob!" cried Janet. Lex smiled a welcome.

They made immediate use of him. They sent him to listen to the complaints of the orphanage director, a fiery young man with a thin mustache. Robert, sitting down, surrounded by boys, riffling through his dictionary every few words, managed to make out that the problem was money, both cash and credit. Supplies were low. The last cook had made off with the radio. Robert wrote down everything the fellow said and then got hustled away to umpire a three-inning softball game. The boys were not adroit. Then Lex arranged an obstacle race. Robert was assigned to hold an inflated clown's hand in front of his chest. This hand had come out of Janet's backpack; she blew it up in three exhalations, her freckles enlarging and then diminishing on her cheeks. Each obstacle racer had to slap the hand; some kids slapped Robert by mistake. Their teeth were as white as Chiclets.

Soon they were corralled into a grim refectory. "Cerca me!" some pleaded. He sat down next to a little beige fellow with reddish hair. All the boys were given crayons and paper. The stuff might have been gold. They drew for half an hour, in blissful silence. Meanwhile Janet examined some inflamed ears—she had an otoscope in her backpack, too. Lex talked with a scowling child in the director's meager office. The child looked less angry after the session.

Robert praised the artwork. He helped the artists print their signatures. The red-haired runt was Miguel O'Reilly. Miguelito was particular about the slant of the apostrophe in his name.

These outcasts—did they know how deprived they were? Lex had told him about them: some abandoned at the gate as infants, some starved and abused before they arrived as toddlers, some rescued from prostitution, or at least reprieved from it. Jaime had served for a while as the mascot of a street gang.

To the boys Robert must seem a patriarch. They were respectful of his Spanish—the stunted vocabulary, the lisp of remote conquerors. They were respectful of his gray hairs, too. In their country a man of his age should already be dead.

The light was reddening, the shadows were lengthening, the parrots would presently lift themselves without a sound from their trees. The afternoon would soon end. Somewhere, elsewhere, maybe in Miami, a congregation was praying together, was feeling united, singular, almost safe.

A child with a birthmark asked to inspect his watch, looked at it gravely, then returned it with a smile. Two others insisted on showing him their dormitory. He peered under the iron cots; he was supposed to laugh at something there, though all he could see was dust. Perhaps a mouse had recently scampered.

He sat down heavily on a cot, startling the children. He drew them close, one against each knee. They waited for his wisdom. "Avinu malkenu," he muttered.

A bell rang: dinner. They stiffened. He let them go.

Oh the thin, hard, greedy boyness of them, undersized nomads fixed for a few years in a patch of land at the end of nowhere. Cow shit in the yard. Beans for dinner on the good days.

Jaime had entered all the play. He'd had a very good time.

They walked back to the inn in the dusk. Some of the huts were little stores, Robert now noticed. Dim bulbs shone on canned goods and medicines. Televisions flickered in the remote interiors, illuminating hammocks. How misleading to call this world the Third. It was the Nether.

Lex had packed a cooler of sandwiches and Cokes that morning. "Jaime can't manage a second restaurant in one day," he now explained to his father.

"What was the first?" Robert wondered. Then he remembered, as if from a rich tapestry seen long ago, the smile of the Chilean woman and the knowing supervision of her lime parrots.

"I have enough food for us all," said Lex.

Janet shook her head. "I'm going to take your father to the café."

The café, behind the inn, was an open kitchen and three tables. A couple of men dined together at one of the other tables. No menu: today's offering was chicken in a spicy sauce. Robert hoped his stomach could manage it. He bought a bottle of rotgut wine.

"L'chaim," said Janet.

He raised his eyebrows.

"My great-grandfather's name was Isaac Fink," she said. "He was a peddler who wandered into Minnesota by mistake, and stayed. The family is Lutheran to its backbones. Still . . ."

"Still, you are somewhat Jewish," he said politely. "Skoal."

They spoke of Lex's talent, and of Jaime's eagerness. They spoke of the children they'd seen that afternoon, and of Janet's work. She planned to spend another few years here. "Then a master's in public health,

I think." Her face grew flushed. "I was serious about giving you a back rub."

And perhaps this part-Jew would be willing also to inspect his tongue and massage his weary abdomen. He had assumed she was lesbian. She probably *was* lesbian. One could be something of everything here. "Thanks, but no," he said. "It's Yom Kippur night."

"Oh, I see," was her bewildered response.

In bed alone he found himself wondering whether the handsome Chilean chef might also be a little bit Jewish. And that native Canadian woman from last night's party—such an expert kvetch. He and Lex should have searched harder for eight more Jews. In a room behind a tailor shop in some town lived a pious old man, too poor to have fled to Miami. In one of the squalid barrios a half-Jewish half-doctor dealt in abortifacient herbs. Atop a donkey, yarmulke concealed by a sombrero, a wanderer sold tin pans. The entire population could be Jewish, Jaime included: people descended from Indians who worshiped quetzal —what was a quetzal but a bird with a schnozz?—and from haughty Marranos who prayed to Yahweh in the basements of basements.

The next morning found him at last master of his bowels. He packed his overnight case and walked across the square to the crumbling church. Inside, though Christ on the wooden cross was naked, plaster saints wore velvet robes. The townspeople too seemed dressed up. He spotted one of the men he'd seen in the café last night. Today the man was sporting the yellow jacket of a gaucho.

Robert sat near the back and listened to the Mass. The sermon began. He did not attempt to understand it, though the Spanish was slow and simple, and the subject was *misericordia,* mercy. *Rachamim.* He thought about Lex, now packing the Jeep for the day's trip to more orphanages. Lex was settling the bill, too. "This trip's on me," he'd said, refusing Robert's money. An admirable, disappointing fellow. *May you too have a son like mine,* Robert thought—the old curse, the old blessing.

A small hand fell on his arm. He twisted his head and saw Jaime. The child danced away, then turned and stood in the open double doorway. Behind him was the treeless square; behind that was the inn, some other houses, the rising hills.

"Ob," Jaime hissed. "Ob!" and he flapped his hand as if warding off a nuisance. Get lost, he seemed to say. Come here, he meant to say. Robert knew the difference, now.

Ob. *Ab. Abba,* father, Abraham. *The father of a multitude of nations have I made thee.* Have you? Through whom? Through Maureen Mulloy, a half-Mick? Through Jaime Katz, an indigenous person?

A multitude of nations: what a vainglorious idea. No wonder we are always in trouble. How about a few good-enough places? he said silently to the priest, to the Christ, to the God rustling in his ear. How about a people that takes care of its children, even those springing from unexalted seed . . .

"Ob!"

Robert rose. He followed his grandson out of the dark, merciful church and into the harsh light of this world.

THE NONCOMBATANT

"If they finish up the war I'll never be a nurse," complained his oldest daughter.

"Why not?" asked Richard.

"There won't be any more battles," she said. She frowned at him from the foot of his bed. He remembered that she was reading a child's biography of Florence Nightingale: she must see herself gliding from tent to tent in the dusty Crimea, bringing comfort to brave British tommies.

"You could be a peacetime nurse," he said. "Like the ones who helped me when I was operated on." In fact he had not found them helpful, those pitying, red-armed women. He had metastatic cancer. He was forty-nine.

". . . nurses in the hospital, Uglies," this uncompromising eight-year-old was saying. "*Will* the war get over?"

"Yes." The war in Europe was already over. Now, in the beginning of July 1945, the war in Asia was winding down. Richard heard exultation in radio commentators' voices. He saw relief on servicemen's faces. His family had arrived in this little Cape Cod town three days ago, and when that afternoon Catherine ran from the parked car into the grocery store for some milk and bread, two young soldiers, safe now from battle, had felt as free as schoolboys to whistle. Richard had watched from behind the windshield.

Though he no longer shared their hunger, he understood it. In her little cotton dresses Catherine was indeed very pretty. The two lines of worry that stood guard between her brows enhanced the softness of her large brown eyes. She had been raised as a Quaker, and she retained the stillness she had learned as a child. She was fifteen years younger than he.

Their two younger daughters were Catherine's replicas. The oldest, this fierce girl who wanted the war to continue, resembled him. She had his narrow pewter eyes and fair skin. "If I can't be an army nurse, I'm going to be a doctor, like you," she said.

"A good second choice," he commended. He saw that her face had already been made rosy by summer, whereas his, he knew, was still pale as sand.

But by the second week of July he was beginning to look better. Within his body there seemed to be a temporary lull in combat. Since coming here he had been able to reduce his painkillers. That made him more alert. Waking up was no fun, but by ten in the morning he could sit more or less comfortably on the screened porch of their rented house. He watched his children playing under a low, gnarled tree. He answered mail he'd received during the recent hospitalization. He listened to Catherine's fluting commentary as, near him on the porch, she sorted laundry, or peeled potatoes, or bent over the jigsaw puzzle.

Every afternoon Catherine walked with the girls to the beach. He watched them until they were out of sight, then picked his way back to the dining room turned sickroom. His bed was here because the bathroom was on this floor—near, though not always near enough. By the time the family returned he'd be waiting for them on the porch. Catherine sometimes carried the three-year-old. She'd remind the older girls to run around to the back of the house and wash their feet under the tap. "And don't make too much noise. Think of Mrs. Hazelton!"

Most days Mrs. Hazelton wasn't there to be thought of. The girls knew she was absent when her bicycle wasn't leaning against her shed. Whenever the bike was gone (they told their parents) they felt free to peer into Mrs. Hazelton's window and announce to each other—and later to anyone who'd listen—the marvels inside. Richard remembered the first day of this inventory: how eagerly they had interrupted each other, the eight-year-old and the six-year-old.

"A teeny, tiny sink, and . . ."

"One bed. A puffy blanket?"

"Comforter," said the attentive Catherine.

"A kettle. Gold?"

"Copper, I'm afraid," said Catherine, smiling.

"A rocking chair. A bureau. A rug like a snake?"

". . . Ah. Braided."

"A black stove-thing, fat."

"That's for cooking children," Richard teased.

"Oh, Daddy," said the oldest, and "She's not a witch," said the middle. But the youngest cried. She had been ready to cry anyway, regarding some other matter. "Mrs. Hazelton is a good witch," Richard explained.

But she might have been the wickedest witch, for all Richard and Catherine knew. They knew only that their landlady was a recent widow and that she worked at the library. They knew that she was tall and spindly; they guessed she was about Richard's age. Her hair was striped with gray and somewhat wild, as if she were standing on a bridge in a windstorm. She wore government issue pants and men's shirts open at the throat.

"There are pictures on her bureau," the girls told him.

"Pictures of what?" he idly inquired.

"*You* know, Daddy. People's faces."

"Photographs?"

"Yup," said the middle daughter. "Men. They all wear caps with sivers."

A few minutes later: "Sivers?" he asked.

"Visors," explained the oldest.

The one-room, one-windowed shed that Mrs. Hazelton retired to while renting her house stood in the northeast corner of the backyard, separated from the family by the victory garden of tomatoes, beans, and lettuce. "There'll be squash after we go home, and pumpkins last of all," said Catherine, grinning at this future abundance. Mrs. Hazelton left vegetables for them in a basket on the back steps. Once in a while they saw her on hands and knees, yanking weeds out of the soil. She wore an overlarge officer's cap. Occasionally they caught sight of her leaving in the morning or returning in the early evening. But often the bike was still gone at nine o'clock, when the littlest girl was fast asleep and the older ones were in bed with their books. And sometimes it wasn't until midnight that Richard, himself reading in his downstairs bed until the hour of the final medication, heard wheels crunch on unyielding soil. He'd look up from the page and wait for the second sound. There: the slam of the little house's door.

By the third week in July he felt well enough to walk to Main Street and back every evening before dinner. In the beginning he walked between his two older children. Then one day he took the youngest along, too, in the old-fashioned stroller that allowed child to face parent, that allowed this parent to gaze at the sweetness of dark brown eyes and the arabesque of lips. He never again left the little look-alike behind.

By the end of July he was taking two walks a day—the one before dinner with all his daughters, and a later one alone, under a sky still patrolled by searchlights. On the first of these nights on the town he had stopped at a pink ice-cream parlor. Working girls sat at tiny round tables. Groups of women and children ate enormous sundaes. The pain within him, never altogether absent, flared. He blamed the harem atmosphere of the place.

The next night he went to a bar. Though he was not much of a drinker, he felt immediately comfortable. Here the walls were of no particular shade, and the dark booths sheltered both military and civilian customers. The radio gave them news from the Pacific. He sat at the counter, making one beer last a long time, testing his pain. The pain did not worsen, as if demonstrating that it could be merciful. Main Street was still busy when he emerged, but his own street was dark. Halfway home he urinated in the shelter of some stunted pines.

Catherine laughed when she smelled beer on his breath. "You old lush."

"I'm celebrating."

"Are you!" she said in her sweet melodious way, while a different tune twanged between them: What on earth have *we* got to celebrate?

There were visits. Banice Bass came, recently discharged from the navy. (Richard had preferred the army. He might have been a major by now. But the military hadn't wanted a sick, overage doctor, even one in remission, and certainly not one with a pregnant wife.)

The MacKechnies and their four children recklessly used up gas coupons to drive from Providence. Rationing would end soon, they all agreed. Catherine was saving drippings in a can on the back of the range, but that too would no longer be necessary. "The war will stop, and my battle will begin," he said to Mac on the porch.

"Cobalt," said Mac right away.

"Yes, we'll try cobalt," sighed Richard. And he would volunteer for an experimental protocol and hope he wasn't put in the placebo group.

It was raining. The wives had taken all the girls to a Betty Hutton movie. The MacKechnie boys grumbled quietly over the jigsaw puzzle. Boughs shifted and leaves rustled under the onslaught of rain. There was thunder in the distance and the hoot of ships. Without making a sound a figure pedaled down the strip of earth that was her own path, and onto the street. She wore no rain jacket, no hat. She lifted her wet head; she biked urgently toward the storm, as if it, at least, loved her.

The bartender, Larry, was a friendly chap. The three or four regulars were also decent fellows. Their talk was always of the end of the war—how long do we have to wait, for Christ's sake; how many more of us need to be lost? A faded, stringy couple usually occupied one of the middle booths. A group of high-spirited middle-aged women often commandeered a table in the back of the room. One had artificially black curls. Another wore a lot of red. A third had a swishy sort of glamour; she could have played Rita Hayworth's aunt in the movies. One night they brought along a new woman. She had untidy hair and a mannish way of dressing . . . He nodded down the length of the bar. Mrs. Hazelton nodded back.

The nods were exchanged on subsequent but not consecutive nights. Sometimes she was there, sometimes she wasn't.

Richard's brother came to visit. Their families were close. His brother's children were old enough to appreciate the gravity of their uncle's situation. A mishap occurred: after lunch his middle daughter fell out of the tree. She blacked out for a moment. Richard's brother, also a doctor, examined her thoroughly—Richard and Catherine anxiously held hands—and pronounced her unhurt. But everybody was shaken. And then, just before dinner, they discovered a puddle under the refrigerator. The food was still edible, but the interior was warming.

Catherine knocked on Mrs. Hazelton's door. No answer. So the sisters-in-law prepared the meal, and the nine of them were already on the porch, eating their salad and hot dogs and corn ("The butter is *supposed* to be melted," the middle girl pointed out) when Mrs. Hazelton cycled past. "We'll get her," said his children, scrambling from the porch.

She was indeed a witch, if cleverness with stubborn household servants was any test. He watched from the kitchen doorway. Catherine sat at the table. Mrs. Hazelton opened a low door that revealed the refrigerator's innards. Then she squatted before it, reaching in to twist something and pull something else. Presently a buzzing indicated that the machinery was working again. She beckoned to Catherine. They examined the refrigerator together, buttocks on heels. Why had she chosen Catherine to instruct? he wondered. Wasn't he the officer here? Both women rose: the graceful younger one in a dotted dress and the angular older one in her dead husband's garments; and they turned toward each other, then toward him. For a moment they loomed larger than life: Grave Acceptance and her grim sister Defiance. Then they became two people again: sweet Cathy and the backyard widow. Her eyes, blue as a gas flame, flickered at him.

August began. His pain decreased. He wasn't deceived, but he took advantage of the situation. One night they hired a babysitter and saw a movie. Another night they went out to dinner. Catherine's charm almost distracted him. How lucky he had been in her, and in their children, and in his work—and yet how willingly he would trade the pleasures of this particular life for life itself. He would hide in a cave, he would skulk in an alley, he would harness himself to a plow—anything, to remain alive.

On August 6 the bar radio shouted out the news of Hiroshima. Many of the patrons applauded. People stood rounds of drinks for each other. Mrs. Hazelton turned from her companions and stared at Richard. Her palms lay flat against her thighs, as if they were lashed there.

On August 9 the destruction of Nagasaki was announced. Mrs. Hazelton was not present. Richard left early. At home he found Catherine knitting by the radio. She turned her large eyes toward him. "This is terrible," she said.

"All wars are terrible." He lowered himself to the floor near her feet. "The bombs may end the war and save lives. Killing to cure, darling." They listened together to the radio's ceaseless gloat.

During the next few days the town swelled with civilians and servicemen asking one another for news from Japan. On August 10 Richard and the girls could hardly make their way through the sidewalk crowds on Main Street. A woman they didn't know, wearing a ruffled turquoise sundress, bent over the stroller and emotionally kissed his youngest daughter, all so fast that the child merely stared instead of crying.

Catherine reported that the beach was packed. A noisy blimp hovered over the water on August 11, enchanting some children and terrifying others. Eventually it moved slowly westward and out of sight. Meanwhile a new concessionaire had appeared, a vendor of cotton candy, which he swirled out of a vat. The girls had never seen such stuff before. When they came home their cheeks were laced with fine pink lines like the faces of alcoholics.

On August 13 the bar was so full that Richard could find no stool. It was better anyway to drink standing. His pain had sharpened again. The underweight elderly couple shared their booth with strangers. Larry was very busy. His son was working, too . . . a wiry young teenager whose presence behind the counter was buoyantly illegal.

On the afternoon of August 14 Richard felt restless. After his family left for the beach he walked to Main Street. The bar was open, and all the regulars were there. Larry and his son had attached tan and peach crepe paper streamers to the center of the ceiling. Then they had twisted the streamers and tacked their ends high on the walls. The carnival effect was spoiled by the lingerie hues. "All the red, white, and blue ones were sold," Larry explained. Some of the streamers became dislodged and hung down like flypaper. The place grew more and more packed. Seven or eight people crowded into each booth. The lively women had already installed themselves in the back of the room. They had acquired some men—a couple of officers and a fellow with a dog collar. Mrs. Hazelton was not among the party.

The air was stifling. Richard took his glass to the doorway, but the frequent comings and goings jostled him, so he went onto the street with his drink—another illegality. He saw a sailor openly fondling a woman's breasts. He saw three others sharing a bottle on a bench. They were committing this breach right in front of the public library, diagonally across the street from Richard. On the third floor of the Woolworth building—the only building in town even to have a third floor—figures were bobbing about at the windows, throwing confetti. The card shop was full of boisterous customers. The tobacco shop, the drugstore . . .

Someone, somewhere, set off a firecracker, then a string of them. Meanwhile the noise in the bar behind him had become a steady roar. "Victory!" he heard. "Defeat!" he heard. "Surrender!" he heard. Laughter thickened. Church bells began to ring—from the Episcopalians at one end of town and from the Congregationalists at the other. Automobiles blared their horns, though there were no automobiles moving on the street, since the street was filling with people—all sizes and ages of people, all shades of clothing and hair; people singing, shouting, hugging, crying, dancing alone and in pairs and in threes and in groups. Someone was playing an accordion. Someone was blowing a trumpet. An army truck poked its nose into the street from a side road, backed up, disappeared. Then a squad of soldiers arrived, not to contain the revelry but to join it, for this was the end of the war, and everyone was part of the glory. A small boy all by himself wandered crying into Richard's view and then was snatched up by someone, presumably his mother, though she looked like yesterday's lady in turquoise. Were the police opening the jails? Was that the meaning of the latest siren? He leaned against the window of the bar and noticed that he still held his half-full glass. He undid one of the lower buttons of his shirt and poured the beer into his garments. It spread onto his stomach. Some of it dripped below his loose waistband and cooled his abdomen, failing to quench the fire within, but diminishing it a little bit, for a little while. He threw the glass into a trash barrel.

From the grocery on the other side of the street came shouts and cheers. From the barbershop, from the dentist's office. Someone was running along the library path, past the three sailors on the bench— but there were twenty people on the bench by now, there were thirty! She raced slantwise toward him, crossing the street without seeing its inebriates. Her hair streamed backward like a figurehead's. He saw that she was not laughing, not crying, not shouting, not delirious with delight. She was raging. Her fury was finally unleashed. He caught her as she tried to run past. She gasped, tensed, raised her fists. Then she recognized him, and threw herself moaning into his embrace. They stood like tens of thousands of celebrants across their mad nation, locked in victory. He felt his dying staunched by her wrath, her passionate unsubmissiveness. It was as if she were a savage new drug, untried, unproven: a last desperate chance. She arched her back and gazed at him for a moment, her blue flames seeming to lick his forehead, his nose, his chin, his forehead again—though perhaps she was merely avoiding looking anywhere else, down at his soggy trousers, for instance, whose wetness she could surely feel through her own. Then she turned her head rapidly from side to side, making her hair shake with the force of the refusal. He released her. She flew into their bar. He slogged toward home, drenched, but not defeated, not yet defeated, not yet.

SETTLERS

~~~~~~

One Sunday morning at eight o'clock Peter Loy stood on the corner of Congdon Street and Brighton Avenue, waiting for the bus downtown. It was October, and the wind was strong enough to ruffle the curbside litter and to make Peter's coat flap about his knees, open and closed, open and closed. He wouldn't have been sorry if the wind had removed the coat altogether, like a disapproving valet. It had been a mistake, this long glen plaid garment with a capelet, suitable for some theatrical undergraduate, not for an ex-schoolteacher of sixty-odd years. He had thought that with his height and thinness and long-ish hair he'd look like Sherlock Holmes when wearing it. Instead, he looked like a dowager.

It didn't matter; this was not a neighborhood that could afford to frown on oddities. Congdon Street was home to an assortment of students, foreigners, and old people. A young couple with matching brief-cases had recently bought one of the peeling houses in the hope that the street would turn chic; they spent all their free time gamely strip-ping paint from the interiors. On weekday mornings white-haired women in bathrobes stared from apartment windows while their middle-aged daughters straggled off to work, and then kept on staring.

The immobility of the stay-at-home mothers suggested that their daughters had locked them in; but often at noontime Peter would see one of them moving toward the corner. Her steps lightened as she neared Brighton Avenue. Here was life! Fresh fish, fish-and-chips, Fishberg the optician . . . Also on Congdon Street was a three-story frame building with huge pillars and sagging porches—a vaguely Southern edifice. Inside lived an entire village of Cambodians.

Peter had moved to this seedy section of Boston three years ago, upon his retirement from the private boys' academy where he'd taught English. His plain apartment here pleased him far more than his aunt's town house in Back Bay. He had dragged out several decades in that town house, first as his aunt's pampered guest and then as her legatee. He had sold it for a good price to the young self-made millionaire next door, Geronimus Barron. No one had hurried Peter out after the sale, though he was eager enough to leave; but within a month of his departure Barron had knocked down the wall between the houses, gutted entire floors, and installed solar panels and skylights. The magnificent place that resulted was featured in *Architectural Digest* and the *New York Times*. The lovely tiled fireplace in his own bedroom, Peter noted with pride, remained untouched.

The bus came. The few passengers aboard already looked fatigued. Peter, his own heart light under his silly coat, began the weekly journey.

"How's the research?" Meg Wren was asking, a few hours later.

Jack and the three children were playing with a soccer ball in the field in back of the house. The field sloped gently toward the woods. A mile away was the Sudbury River. Peter couldn't see the river now, from the kitchen, but he could glimpse it from the third-floor guest room where he stayed whenever he spent the night.

"I'm having trouble placing Mrs. Jellyby," Peter said.

"Mrs. Jellyby?" Meg repeated, wrinkling her long brow.

Peter waited. Her blue gaze was intelligent, but he was not sure exactly how well read she was. She had been born and raised in Wisconsin and had come East after college, almost fifteen years ago, and had quickly married one of his former students. "*Bleak House?*" she said.

"*Bleak House,*" Peter commended. "Mrs. Jellyby is the crackpot who spends all her time collecting money for the natives of Borrioboola-Gha. Her own ragged children keep tumbling down the stairs. Their house is filthy and falling apart. 'Never have a mission,' her poor husband warns the heroine. These days we would applaud Mrs. Jellyby's selflessness. We'd be glad to know that she cares about Africa—funny how some things never change."

"'Ye have the poor always with you'?"

"Yes, and they're always the same poor. Mrs. Jellyby carries her ardor to excess and neglects the need nearest her. Not a very Christian form of charity."

Peter paused. He had been lecturing to Meg, taking advantage of her daughterly attention. In years spent among self-important high school teachers and garrulous old ladies, he had accustomed himself to the listener's role. Now he had found someone who listened as attentively as he did. It was as if she had inherited the talent from him—or, since that was impossible, had caught it. And this house of hers—so old, and so fresh—it too seemed to want to hear what he had to say. "Mrs. Jellyby's philanthropy isn't very Jewish, either," he went on. "You could make a case that her charity is in Maimonides' seventh degree—she doesn't know the names of the people she's relieving and they've certainly never heard of her. But Dickens meant her to be a figure of fun, and he keeps arguing with me. He says that Maimonides was talking about charity closer to home, and that Mrs. Jellyby doesn't qualify at all . . . I do get a bit carried away, don't I?"

Meg was silent. Of all the silences he had ever experienced, Meg's was his favorite. It was not disappointed, like his mother's; not bored, like those of the women he had courted; not embarrassed, like that of the search committee that had failed to award him the headmastership; not sleepy, like students in late afternoon remedial classes; and not terrifying, like his mute aunt after her stroke.

"I think you're enjoying this task," she said after a while.

"Carrot scraping?" he smiled. He had been scraping carrots for her while they—he—talked.

"Thinking about Dickens and Maimonides," she said. "Finding Maimonides' eight levels of charity in the novels of Dickens," she carefully amended. "It does sound . . . nice. I knew you were interested in Dickens. But I didn't know you were interested in Judaism."

"I'm not interested in Judaism. Only in Jews. They're so complicated . . ."

"Yes."

". . . always have been." At Harvard just after the war he had noticed that his brightest classmates were the Jewish boys. They were at home with Swift's grotesques and Jane Austen's ingenues. Mastering Middle English was a snap after Hebrew. Shakespeare's tales were just another set of Midrashim. Every exchange with one of those students had left Peter admiring and envious. He wondered what encounters Meg had thus far endured—dinner party debate? Lordly attempts at seduction? . . . And here was her husband, open-faced, steady as the junior high school principal he was. He walked in grinning, his arm outstretched.

The three children bounded in behind Jack: two boys and a little girl. The younger boy's hair matched the pumpkin on the windowsill. Meg said that his coloring came from her side of the family, though her own smooth hair was brown. The children greeted Peter lightly, as if a week had not gone by since they last saw him; as if he hadn't spent over an hour on bus, trolley, and little train; as if he lived there always.

Someday he must really live there, Meg had said more than once. The third-floor room was just the place to retire from his retirement.

After lunch the three adults drank hot cider under an apple tree and talked about the children.

"They're lazy," said Jack. "I tried to teach Ned chess the other day. Too difficult, he said. Checkers is good enough for him."

Meg said, "It's good enough for a lot of people."

"Oh, Meg. We send them to private schools. We shore up this old house for them." He wasn't complaining, Peter noticed; he was proud.

"You spend two hours a day commuting," Meg added.

"I do. So they've got to," said Jack.

"Got to what?" she laughed.

"Play chess." And he laughed, too. "What do you think, Peter?"

"What do I think about what?" Peter hedged.

"About our three hooligans. About the worth of private education. About the country life." Jack breathed deeply. Generations of farmers and ministers expressed themselves in that pleased inhalation. The house had always been in his family; some ancestor had built it. A century ago he would have farmed the land with his sons and a few hired hands. They would have made a genteel go of it. The boys would have gone to Harvard as a matter of course. Now he had to weary himself every day at a profession he was unfit for, and his children would have to compete for college places against the grandchildren of longshoremen and pullman porters. To strengthen them for the fight, Meg drove them to their Cambridge school every morning and home again in the late afternoon. In the interval she worked as a programmer, also in Cambridge.

Peter said, "I think the house is its own reward."

The stone wall in the garden was mauve under the afternoon sun. The kitchen windows gleamed like water. Roses bloomed with a soft fire—there would be one or two still glowing as late as Thanksgiving, Peter remembered—and zinnias and asters flourished along the path to the door. It was a house to come home to. That the young Wrens were inside watching television seemed not hopeless, just sad. Meg's modesty and Jack's busyness perhaps did not perfectly serve their offspring.

"Children tend toward the mean," Peter suggested.

"The mean and nasty," said Jack. But Meg said doubtfully, "The mean between Jack and me?"

"The mean of their own generation," said Peter, smiling.

"Is that unavoidable?" she said, not smiling.

He didn't like to drive, didn't own a car, but if he lived here he could drive the kids to school and back, and Meg could work at home. She was a valued programmer; her company would allow her that privilege; these days any arrangement was possible. And eventually his aunt's legacy, unexhausted, would go to the children.

In the mornings the young of Congdon Street went off to school, the bigger ones shepherding the smaller. Even the smallest had pilgrim backpacks. Some mothers walked along behind, not interfering, just watchful. Peter wondered if the women took turns as monitors. The daytime danger was from traffic. Peter too kept an eye on the children from his window. Sometimes, out early to buy the paper, he found himself in their midst; a little crowd of small Asians and Central Americans would divide briefly for his sake and then reunite behind him. He felt like a Maypole. The children wore every shade of corduroy. How were they faring in the Land of Opportunity? he wondered. The manager of the Cambodian building, N. Gordon, was being brought to court because of his failure to maintain the building properly. The failure was not his fault, his lawyer had countered; the place was overcrowded; these people kept subrenting to one another.

Peter went out every day. He now recognized some of the slow-moving white-haired women, and smiled at them. He used the main library downtown. He read a book about Dickens and Sabbatarians and another about Dickens and Jews. Sometimes he met a colleague or a former student for lunch. He went to afternoon movies and sat in the back row with his long legs on the seat in front of him. He went to friends' houses for dinner, or fixed himself healthful meals at home.

The Wrens gave an annual afternoon party on the Sunday after the game. Meg did the work herself, with some assistance from the family and from Peter. She baked cheddar cheese puffs. She twisted salami into flutes and arranged crudités around a bowl of yogurt. Peter remembered his aunt's cook's zealously constructed trifles, each layer less edible than the one before. Meg's canapés were at least tasty.

That morning Peter stood at the kitchen counter, spreading fish paste onto little squares of pumpernickel and admiring the view out the window. A stand of spruces made him think of Christmas. Beside him, Meg sliced cucumbers. They were both wearing jeans; both had a birch-tree litheness; he might have been her older brother.

The crowd at the party was, as always, varied—local gentry, old friends, co-workers, a pair of ancient female cousins of Jack's. Also there was a group of parents from the children's school, including two notables, both Jews: a psychologist who was also a TV commentator, and Geronimus Barron, Peter's former neighbor. Their wives were not particularly attractive, just assured. A generation ago, Peter reflected, Jewish wives had been well dressed and cultivated and full of leisure. Now they were all practicing medicine. You couldn't keep up with people like that.

He was popular at this party. People remembered him from year to year. A friend of Meg's whose husband was leaving her had once wept on his shoulder in the pantry. That couple seemed to have reconciled, he noticed. The Wrens's dentist fancied himself a devotee of Dickens, although Peter was under the impression that he had read only *Oliver Twist*. The cousins made much of him. "We'd like to talk to you more often than once in a blue moon."

"Would be lovely," he said.

"We'll have to get Peggy to arrange it."

Peggy? " . . . happy families are *not* alike," someone was saying.

" . . . more to be pitied than censored. She snoops to conquer." Who was that punster? Oh, the TV psychologist . . . And somehow Geronimus Barron was at his side. How long had he been standing there?

"It's nice to see you again, Mr. Loy."

"Peter," Peter corrected. "I didn't hear you come up, Geronimus. You were as quiet as a tiger."

"Is that what a corporate takeover feels like?" asked one of the cousins.

"I don't know," said Geronimus Barron. He had a habit of answering as precisely as possible whatever question had been posed. This gave him an obedient air. "I don't want to take you over, Mr. Loy, Peter, but I wish you were part of my staff. Margaret says that you're the last of the lucid thinkers."

Margaret? Geronimus, hands in pockets, smiled a courteous refusal to the teenager passing a tray of wine. The cousins, as if to make amends for so abstemious a guest, took two glasses each. How old was this quiet tycoon, Peter wondered. Forty? You could put him naked and empty-handed on a desert island, and in five years he'd be chief minister to the native king. Maimonides had risen to court physician in record time . . . "What else does Margaret say?"

"Peggy never talks much," said one cousin.

"Still waters run deep," said the other.

"She and I serve together on the scholarship committee," said Geronimus, and the talk turned to minority recruitment. Peter had just received the latest bulletin from the boarding school he himself had attended. The school had recently invited two South Bronx boys to study there; and two unhappier faces had never before been immortalized on high quality vellum. Entrapment, Peter called it. Geronimus listened.

The next morning Meg said that she would drop the children at school before leaving Peter at Harvard Square. Peter was pleased to be part of this family ritual. A curved line of automobiles humped forward slowly. Only one car at a time was allowed to disburden itself. The students getting out of the cars had the ragamuffin look of the rich. Meg wore a ski sweater and did not look rich, just wholesome. "Think of Jack's long drive every day," she was saying as they left the school grounds. "It's no wonder he can't finish his doctorate—he spends all his time on the highway. Sometimes I think we should splurge on a chauffeur. It would give Jack two more hours a day to work on his thesis. He could sit in the backseat with a laptop. Is that mad?"

"On the contrary. It's innovative. It's the sort of solution Geronimus Barron would think up."

"Is it? Jack won't hear of it."

"Give him time." He glanced at her worried profile. "Jack is flexible," he said. But that was a lie. Jack was rigid. He, Peter, was the flexible one. His was a flexibility achieved late in life, after unhappiness and disappointment, and he was proud of it. Postponed achievements were perhaps the best. Maimonides had married for the first time in late middle age, and had even sired a son . . . Meg turned toward him with a warm, even a marital smile. "I wish I could take you all the way to your apartment, but I have an early conference."

"I have to go to Widener," he lied again.

She pulled up near one of the Yard gates. Peter opened the door.

"My dear," he said.

"*My* dear," she said, charmingly. She waited for him to get out and slam the door. Then she drove away.

One night in December there was a fire in the Cambodian building. Some woman had created a makeshift barbecue on her kitchen floor because the stove no longer worked or the gas had been shut off. Not much damage resulted, and nobody was forced to relocate, but for an hour all of the building's inhabitants stood in the street like the little band of refugees they were. When the firemen announced that it was safe to reenter the building, they filed in. Peter, watching from his window, would have liked to have invited some of them for a cup of tea, but which ones? He wished Meg were beside him in her quilted robe.

It was the Friday night before Christmas. Weak electric candles burned in some windows, and the hopeful young couple had installed a tree in their living room, but they were in Stowe and the tree's lights were out. The rest of the street was unfestive. Peter's apartment, the exception, was glowing—he loved Friday nights; even though he no longer had a job he still felt an end-of-the-week release—but the shivering presence of Jack Wren was robbing his place of warmth. The man had stayed late at school to make sure everything was in order before vacation, like a proper principal, and then he had driven straight into Boston with all the Friday night traffic, straight to Peter. He had arrived at seven o'clock. It was now after eight. Peter kept idiotically offering him food. Jack kept refusing. He would go home soon, he kept saying. He and Meg had not separated yet. They had not told the children. They were still man and wife. Meg was expecting him. "It's unbelievable," he said.

Not to mention unseemly, Peter thought. Also untrustworthy. And what was Geronimus Barron planning to do about his own wife? But he knew the answer to that question. Mrs. Barron—properly, Dr. Barron—was a distinguished immunologist; plenty of scientists were no doubt eager to keep her company. Geronimus too seemed to like her. Theirs had been a good marriage, Peter realized. They would part as friends.

But what about the Wren children? he asked himself, rattled. How would they fare on the inevitable vacation when they were forced to share a villa or a yacht—or, more likely, a tent and a latrine—with the overachieving Barron kids? Well, maybe the Barron children too tended toward the mean. Jews were subject to the same genetic laws as everybody else, Peter reasoned. Jews were . . .

Jack said, "They take our jobs, our money, our positions at schools. They take over our towns. Now they are taking our women."

"Not our houses," Peter murmured. "Not all our houses."

"Meg never liked our house."

"No, Jack. Maybe she says that now, but . . ."

"She always said it." Jack pressed his nose against the window like one of his sons. "She would have preferred to live in some split-level in the boonies and send the kids to public school. Now I wish we'd done that. She wouldn't have met any Geronimus Barron at the Nothingsville PTA."

Peter had to agree. Which proved, he supposed, that Margaret and Geronimus had been destined for each other. She had once told him that she wasn't meant to be gentry; that she wasn't aristocratic, just simple; and that, despite her ease with computers, she wasn't particularly bright. Nor was she ambitious. They had been alone under the apple tree with her sleeping daughter. When he had opened his mouth to argue with this unexpected and certainly inaccurate disclosure, she had put her finger over his lips. "Just an ordinary prairie girl," she had whispered. He remembered the blinding beauty of her pale freckled face and her blue eyes; and he understood that what she felt for Geronimus was a prairie love, irresistible as the wind.

He moved to Jack's side and put an arm around the younger man. In the supportive embrace, Jack held himself straighter.

"You'll never get over her," said Peter, "but the rage will ease, and the sorrow."

"Yes," said Jack. Peter wondered without much interest who would marry Jack. Some nice woman. She would appreciate the house but would not realize that its furnishings included a retired teacher with a bee in his bonnet about Dickens and Maimonides. Peter would be invited to visit perhaps once a year. As for Geronimus and Meg, they would live in a penthouse overlooking the redeveloped harbor. A caterer would take charge of their hors d'oeuvres. He hoped they would keep him on their party list.

Along the sidewalk below hurried a large man and a tarty looking woman. On the other side of the street two young men walked, arguing. Though they had left their bookbags at home, their beards and their parkas identified them as law students. They would be gone after commencement, Peter predicted; they would decamp for Charlestown or the South End. The hopeful young couple with briefcases, discovering themselves pregnant, would sell their folly and flee to a western suburb. The students' places, the couple's house, would be taken by other people. Homes allowed themselves to be commandeered by whoever came along. Not like cats; cats remain aloof. Not like dogs; dogs remain loyal. Like women, he made himself think, willing misogyny to invade him, to settle in, so that in another few years everybody would assume he had been in its possession forever.

STRANGER IN THE HOUSE

~~~~~~~~~~~~~~~~~~~~~~~~~~~~~~

Avigdor never worried about his first wife's faithfulness. Dahlia was pretty in a hot-eyed, half-groomed way; and at parties she'd been openly flirtatious. He remembered her stance, pelvis forward, hand on hip, sleeveless flowered blouse revealing moist dark underarms. He'd shrugged. He knew she preferred him to other men. And he'd had the confidence of his own seductive powers, and of his youth, too, or at least relative youth. He was only fifty when they divorced—a tall man whom women looked at more than once; a French-born Israeli whose slightly accented Hebrew made them listen, made them move closer . . .

But he was almost sixty now. And his new wife, Sharon, though (in her own smiling words) no spring chicken, aroused in him a jealousy that flared like ardor. Unlike ardor, it didn't exhaust itself. Some devil kept fanning the flame. It burned now, on an early morning that was still cool, though the day would heat up soon enough—wasn't this Jerusalem in July? The breeze that ruffled the ivy on the balcony seemed to refresh Sharon, to refresh Phil; but he, Avigdor, kept on sweating. He sat like a duenna between them, stiff with his shameful fever. His American wife and his American brother exchanged opinions about American movies across his lap. A code, this?—names like Capra and Cukor and Cary Grant; well, he knew Cary Grant, dead wasn't he? but when alive possessed of a dark smoky glance like Phil's, whose brown eyes were staring right now into Sharon's blue ones. In slightly accented English Phil was making some comment about the pursuit of happiness. Another code? Who was Robert Altman?

Avigdor was not an easy man to delude. But Sharon had muddled him the very night they met, almost two years ago, in Phil's own house in Massachusetts. Phil had introduced his brother from Jerusalem to his neighbor, Sharon Levine. *Levine?* Avigdor silently hooted. If this tall, blue-eyed, pearl-haired beauty wasn't an Irishwoman you could cut off his right hand.

But it turned out that Sharon was not only Jewish but halachically Jewish. Her mother—South Boston Irish on both sides—had long ago undergone an Orthodox conversion in order to marry her father, Belkin. The young Sharon Belkin had married a Jewish dentist, Levine, now dead. A kind man, she told him; very possessive, though.

And now she was Sharon Belkin Levine Nathanson. A dragon's tail of Jewish surnames, the face of a Celtic sorceress. And a kind heart too. Monks leaped off cliffs for such women.

"More coffee, Phil?" said Sharon.

"Thanks," Phil said, and handed her his cup. "What neighborhood am I looking at?—that far-off hill."

"Gilo," Avigdor told him. They could see cars in the distance spurting along the roadway from Gilo. Nearby the Boulevard Herzl pulsed, unseen from their quiet curved street. But Avigdor felt the traffic; it set off an unwholesome thudding in his veins. Automobiles would accomplish Jerusalem's ruin more thoroughly than Arabs or Russians or Ethiopians or Americans. "You're looking over at Gilo," he said again. "Dahlia lives there now."

Philippe had never cared for Dahlia. "I'd like to see your children," he said. He was in town for only two days, on his way home from a cancer convention in Athens.

"Good, call them, they'll want to see you too. They come here a lot. They're crazy about Sharon . . ."

"My cooking," she murmured.

". . . crazy about her, like everybody else. Lucky for us both that I'm not a suspicious man." She gazed at him without smiling. "Call them, Phil," he said, ratcheting his heartiness. "The number's pasted on the telephone. Maybe you'll catch them before they leave for classes. Ask them for . . . when, Sharon?"

"Tonight," she said. "Daniel has a lab until five or so."

"Does he." The voice sharp.

"He does." The voice mild.

Phil got up to telephone. Avigdor kissed Sharon. Her mouth was as jammy as a child's. Her hair, silver since the age of eighteen, was swept back from her face and secured by a blue headband. It hung straight and thick almost to her shoulders. He kissed her again. "When will Michael visit us?"

"Next month." Her son was an actor in New York. Her daughter practiced psychology in California. She had a grandchild, too, this enchantress of fifty.

Avigdor was leaving the balcony just as his brother was returning; they had to slide past each other nose to nose. "They're coming tonight," reported Philippe, taking Avigdor's chair. And he was still sitting there fifteen minutes later. His curly head leaned toward Sharon's sleek one. Avigdor, on his way to work, said good-bye to their backs. They turned toward him to echo his words, without apparent guilt.

Their inclined heads shimmered before his eyes as he walked to the bus stop. They must separate soon, he reasoned. Phil had an appointment with a colleague. Sharon had her part-time jobs. Three mornings a week she worked at the Sheridan Institute for Cultural Exchange, a berth for retired diplomats and literary types. Sharon was the institute's liaison with the United States consul. She earned a small salary which, along with a meager income from her husband's estate, she insisted on contributing to their household.

Her afternoon job was unpaid: she worked at an Ethiopian Absorption Center, euphemistically called a hotel. Sharon helped the visiting nurse, soothed the women, played with the children. She had come to believe in their demons and respect their fears. She trusted their notion of physiology, too. Some pains might really be the work of evil spirits, she'd told Avigdor. And perhaps it was true that a miscarriage did not obliterate the infant's soul, that the child lurked in the womb until the next pregnancy. Mother and newborn thrived best if a midwife performed the delivery, she'd informed him with a serious nod. During the eighteen months that Sharon had lived in Jerusalem she had sometimes assisted in sudden labors; she had become a sort of honorary midwife.

"Like a big-city taxi driver," Avigdor told her.

"Maybe I could become one for real."

"A cabbie?"

"A midwife."

"You'd have to study nursing first."

"I could go to nursing school down at Hadassah. I'd take my lunch break in the room with the windows."

The sun pouring through Chagall's ruby and cobalt panes would pool onto her lustrous head, bent over formulas she'd never understand.

"Classes would be conducted in Hebrew," he murmured.

"Nachon," she said, looking hopeful. It was as if a ventriloquist had thrown the word into her mouth. Her Hebrew was pitiful; she used it only with the local Yemenite grocer, who spoke very little English. "I just *ohev* your *tapuzes*," she exclaimed one day to Amon, holding the oranges in her cupped hands as if they were breasts. Avigdor wondered if she had ever granted her favors to a woman. Sharon soldiered on. "My *ba'ali* here, he *ohevs* them also." And little Amon smiled—a smile that was one part subservience and nine parts adoration.

There had been no further talk of midwifery. But Sharon faithfully attended the Ethiopians. The hotel was only a block from their apartment. Hundreds of immigrants lived there. They stayed for months, sometimes a year, before another place was found for them. Busloads of children left for school in the mornings and returned in the afternoons. They played on the roof of a parking garage. Sharon reported that on rainy days they rolled marbles in the echoing lobby.

Sometimes Avigdor would pass a small group of young men on the sidewalk. They wore assorted hoodlum garments—jeans, flannel shirts, knitted caps. They spoke Amharic among themselves. He understood a few words of the soft, genderless language. The verb came last in the sentence. A wag of a newspaper columnist had written that the syntax reflected the temperament of the people: their reluctance to take action until the last moment. (The following week several angry letter writers reviled the columnist.)

Occasionally Avigdor saw women in traditional garments at the bus stop. There was one such woman today. She carried an infant in a sling; a small child clung to her skirt. Patiently they waited. Meekly they boarded the crowded bus and fitted themselves somewhere—he lost sight of them. Such tolerant beings, Sharon had said. They could squat all day long in the corridors of the hotel, outside their narrow rooms, doing absolutely nothing. She collected medical details. Very little hypertension. Plenty of diabetes, though . . .

"They are Jews, after all," he said.

"Some of our friends don't think so."

"The rabbis have spoken."

"They are treated as underpeople," she said. "They are made infants of. They are discouraged from studying anything—the adults, anyway. Functionaries do their shopping for them."

"They learn Hebrew so slowly," he said.

She reddened.

He tried to make amends. "They're not used to cars; our traffic could kill them."

"Their rooms have no kitchen equipment," she said. "They aren't allowed to cook in the communal dining room. Paid workers prepare their meals and they are insulted by that, and insulted by the diet we press on them. They hate our food."

"'Our'?"

She shook her head in annoyance, and rightly; she had adapted to the honey and yogurt and apricots of the Middle East as she had earlier adapted to the pretentious cuisine of her husband the dentist, abandoning the boiled dinner of her mother the convert. But she still sweetened her underwear drawer with her mother's Christmas trick: an orange studded with cloves. She made a new spice ball every week. "Ethiopians gag on our salads," she went on. "In their villages lettuce is fed to horses. It's as if you and I had to eat raw oats."

And now, swinging off the bus at the central station, loping down the Jaffa Road, Avigdor grinned at the image of himself and Sharon feeding out of nosebags. It was his first smile of the day; the jealous spirit that spoiled his pleasure and ruined his temper had at some point jumped off his back.

He walked the six blocks to his building. Cars and busses grunted by; the narrow road was already jammed. He climbed the four flights of stairs to his office and sat down at his too-neat desk. He was an honored emeritus here—shown off to clients, not asked to do much designing. But he paid close attention to projects. They were extending sewers for a new development north of the city. He spread out the plans: white lines and numbers on blue paper, white filaments on blue ice. When Sharon leaned forward to hear Phil's opinions on Elia Kazan, a lock of hair tumbled in front of her morning-glory eyes. The new pipes would gleam as if lined with beryl.

Young engineers dropped in on him. Between visits his thoughts followed his wife. She left the balcony, she dressed for work, she boarded the first bus, she boarded the second, she entered the Cultural Institute. Her head illumined the brown corridors. She settled herself in her little office. The chairman of the board, former minister Shmuel Ben Zion, would soon be knocking on her door. Wouldn't he?

"He sometimes pokes his head in," Sharon had acknowledged. "Poor man; he hasn't enough work to keep him occupied."

"Poor man! Shmuel Ben Zion? Murdered his first two wives; I have it on good authority."

"Murdered?" she laughed.

"Drove them to death with his philandering. Watch out for that goat."

"Poor Shmuel," Sharon insisted. Then she laughed again. "I got mixed up in the beginning, called him Ben."

Avigdor laughed with her, relieved as always by her mild dysfunctional streak. One day he had come home to find Sharon curled in the corner chair next to the stereo, the better to hear a new Brahms disk, though she knew, didn't she, how couldn't she, that the sound from the two speakers converged perfectly on the couch against the other wall.

She'd be sitting at her old-fashioned desk now, her legs wound around each other in the privacy of the kneehole. Philippe must be prowling around some hospital, exchanging dark tales with his fellow oncologists. Dahlia hunched over film in her dirty office. Their children shifted glumly on hard chairs within the fortress of the university.

He left his office in the middle of the afternoon. He got off the bus, bought some irises. Flowers in hand, he stopped at the door of Amon's shop and peered into its dark fastness. The Yemenite was leaning against the shelf of preserves, arms folded across his chest.

"Do we need anything?" Avigdor asked.

Amon flashed his professional twinkle. "Your lady purchased potatoes, carrots, squash . . ."

"Her famous stew."

". . . and oranges. No apricots or figs," Amon added with regret.

She would have bought such delicacies earlier, at the *shuk,* along with beef for the stew. At the *shuk* she moved from stall to stall without avarice. Under powerful bulbs her hair gleamed like a rich sweetmeat. Here one thing hid another—the open selling of hashish screened the secret selling of opium; the oily vendor of halvah owned a factory and lived in splendor; a poultry man purchased secrets for the Iraquis. Only Sharon was what she seemed: a tall, wide-hipped housewife on her way home from work, stopping by to pick up a few things. "People stare at you here, too," he'd murmured into her ear one afternoon when he'd surprised her at work, accompanied her on the bus, escorted her into the bazaar.

"They stare at *us,*" she'd corrected, stopping. He had to stop as well. She leaned her head into his neck. He dropped his hand onto her shoulder. "You particularly," she said. Shoppers jostled them from behind, muttered, stomped around them. But Avigdor and Sharon held their pose, gazing ahead like a couple on shipboard. "Your pirate's complexion," she said. "Your Gallic complexity. Your long legs. Your British tweeds."

"My gorgeous wife," he said, not lovingly.

"Move!" barked a voice at their backs, and so they drifted forward, bride and wary groom.

"Did she buy coffee?" Avigdor now inquired of Amon.

"No."

"We need some."

Amon nodded, but turned his attention first to a black child and her grandmother. They asked for powdered milk, the child interpreting the old woman's Amharic. The old woman picked up the milk and put some coins on the counter. Then she thought of something else. "Tapuzim," translated the child, holding up two fingers. Amon gave the child the oranges. "Bakshish," he smiled, waving away further payment.

Did Sharon get oranges free too? Avigdor sourly watched Amon grind the coffee beans. He walked home, strode up the stone stairs. He remembered the two heads outlined against the pale morning. He banged into the apartment.

He sniffed. The spicy, nutty smell of her stew drifted toward him. He peeked. Languidly she moved from sink to stove. Even at the airport, while Israelis shoved, Sharon merely drifted toward the gate, passively maintaining her position in their midst. He wondered how she'd behave in a fire.

Fresh from the shower, Philippe sat on the living room couch reading the newspaper and listening to Chopin. His shirt of narrow blue and white stripes must have cost a hundred dollars. "You look Parisian," said Avigdor by way of greeting.

"Do I? I feel as American as all get-out."

They had both left France after the war, Avigdor for Palestine, Philippe and their parents for America. "I hate Paris, in fact," Philippe added in an amiable way.

Sharon, entering with a bowl of anemones for the coffee table, said, "I love the gardens there. The flowers."

"Oh the flowers," said Philippe, straightening a blossom.

"Mine," said Avigdor, handing her his irises, upside down.

While they were waiting for the kids, he made cocktails. He made Sharon's too strong and Philippe's too weak. Each complained. When Daniel and Dinah burst in there was a storm of embraces. Daniel wrapped his arms around Sharon from behind and pulled a pack of cigarettes from her apron pocket. Before dinner Dinah and Sharon disappeared into the bedroom for ten minutes and came out rosy and laughing. Avigdor knew that Dinah never confided in her mother. Poor, shunned Dahlia.

At dinner he spoke French to his brother, Hebrew to both kids, Arabic to Dinah, who was studying the language. He said nothing at all to Sharon. After dinner he took his brandy out onto the balcony and stood glowering down into the street where an old Ethiopian woman and a child were hanging about under the lamp.

The kids whisked Philippe off to a new bar.

"Everyone makes use of you," Avigdor said to Sharon. "You're like this damned city."

"You have a choice, Vig," she said, smoking at him in the bedroom. Her blouse, partly unbuttoned, revealed her fragrant breasts. "You can trust me or you cannot. If you choose to trust me, *b'seder.*" She paused. "All right," she translated in a tentative way, as if she was not sure she had properly pronounced the phrase that any wooden-headed tourist could manage. "But if you choose not to trust me," she continued. And then did not continue. Her eyes filled, and she shook her head heavily as if in slow recognition of destiny: the men who loved her would forever doubt her.

She had twice separated from her first husband because of his suffocating attention. Avigdor knew that she was capable of leaving him, too. She would pack up her small wardrobe and her few books;

she would remove her unproductive stock certificates from the safe; she would take an airport bus and idle toward the gate and board a plane. She would rent an apartment in the town she came from; she would get a job; she would serenely begin life again. He knew that to keep her he'd have to ignore the lustful eyes of his brother, of his son, of Amon and Ben Zion and doddering diplomats and guests at cocktail parties and Dinah and men in the street and Cary Grant. He had to trust his wife.

Two weeks later he came home early again. He carried no flowers. He would have picked up fruit and coffee but Amon's shop was closed. Though unencumbered by packages he climbed the stairs slowly. As he fit his key into the lock he heard a voice. The voice, he was certain, came from the bedroom.

"You have a choice," she had told him.

He chose. He chose not to trust her. He turned the key as softly as he could. He entered on tiptoe. He stood briefly in the little hall. The living room was empty, as he had expected.

The voice—it was Sharon's—rose and fell. He could hear the caress in the tones, but he could not understand the words. Moving closer to the door, which was ajar, he could still not make out the sense. And even when he saw the two of them, facing each other cross-legged on the bed, each pricking an orange with cloves, the words remained unfamiliar, though his accomplished ear recognized sounds of love. The little girl, who was facing the door, saw him, and cried "Ah!"—a syllable of surprise in any language. Then the child reached for Sharon's hair. The small dark fingers grasped at the candescent strands, black fire on white fire. Sharon turned her head, though the movement must have hurt her, for the fist still clung. She smiled at her husband—that blameless, ruinous smile—and then turned back to the child. She gently loosened the fingers and spoke several reassuring sentences. Avigdor, though his brain was whirling, realized that what he was listening to was confident, fluent Amharic.

He experienced an warm inner stirring. A man more easily fooled might have mistaken this feeling for admiration, even for love. But he knew that it was only his old jealousy, implacably expanding. Avigdor would now find room in his heart to suspect Ethiopians, every glistening man among them; and their children, too.

Reprinted from TIKKUN MAGAZINE, A BI-MONTHLY JEWISH CRITIQUE OF POLITICS, CULTURE, AND SOCIETY. Subscriptions are $31.00 per year from TIKKUN, 251 West 100th Street, 5th floor, New York, NY 10025.

FELIX'S BUSINESS

One morning at breakfast Lisa said to Felix, "What would happen to you if the postal service went kaput?"

"I'd do business as usual," replied Felix. "Mail is as old as the Ptolemies. If the government abolished the post office department, private couriers would take over."

"But suppose Congress made letter writing illegal."

"I'd drop underground."

Lisa said in a rush, "Suppose correspondence went out of fashion? Litigation is never out of fashion. If you were married to me, you'd always have something to eat."

Felix recognized this as a proposal despite its conditional mood. He was unsurprised by the offer. He said evenly and politely, "Well, let's think about it." So they stacked the dishes and both left for work.

When Felix got to his shop there was already a customer waiting, Dr. Blaker. Wearing his white coat, Dr. Blaker leaned against the doorway like a ruler. He was a slender, handsome man of about fifty who had a busy periodontal practice.

"Good morning," said Felix.

Dr. Blaker shook hands with the young man. "Good morning," he said.

Felix unlocked his door and went into the shop and threw his hat at a peg on the wall. The hat missed. He bent over and picked it up and threw it again, and this time it landed on the peg. (The hat was invisible and all the business with it was pantomime. Felix didn't own a hat. But detectives and hometown newspaper editors and other people in small chambers always tossed their hats onto pegs; it seemed to put clients at ease.)

After the second, successful attempt, Felix withdrew a letter from the top drawer of the desk. He handed the letter to Dr. Blaker, who had seated himself in the customer's chair. Felix sat down in his own chair and swiveled it away from the desk so that he faced his client. There was nothing on the desk anyway but a cumbersome nonportable Royal.

Darling,

You're finding it hard to remember what you were like twenty-five years ago? Then let me tell you what you were like. You had a headful of yellow curls and a brainful of swept-up notions, like wood shavings. Adorable. One day you fluttered down beside me in Ideas of Western Literature, and you gave me the greatest, greatest gift: you let me relax. I hadn't realized that one could relax with a Girl, but you were so funny and decent and responsive. The you-that-was is embedded in my memory for all time. I could pick your eighteen-year-old self out of a lineup in a minute, *this* minute.

Forever,

Dr. Blaker gave the letter his attention, and Felix gave the doctor *his* attention. For six months Dr. Blaker had been writing to this Darling, whom he had not seen for almost a quarter of a century. Nor would he agree to see her now; though she, half a continent away, urged that they meet in some neutral place. Dr. Blaker turned thumbs down on reunion. He wanted to be a correspondent, he had said at their first interview, not a co-respondent. Felix had then understood that his customer was bound to the conventions of courtly love, and that theirs would be a long and profitable alliance. (He still thought so, despite Lisa's breakfast-table warnings.)

Dr. Blaker put the letter in his pocket. "Thank you," he said. He stood up and gave Felix a grateful look.

Felix stood too. "Chivalry is always congenial," he said, and bowed his client out.

So much was congenial in this trade. Felix took off his horn-rimmed glasses and, wincing, fit a pair of wire spectacles to his ears. He rolled a sheet of paper into his typewriter and began to type.

Many versions and many rollings later, Felix thrust away all drafts but the last:

> Dear Dad,
>
> Thanks for your note. The check must have dropped out. I *am* considering law school, just as you suggested, but first I must complete my training as a bar mitzvah ventriloquist. Or maybe you neglected to put the check in. The coach says I would also make a terrific rental mourner. Or maybe you omitted making it out (the check, I mean). It cannot be that you are generous only to those of your sons who follow more or less in your footsteps, and that you prefer to write off (but not write off checks to) the runt of the litter, the dreamer, the (shall we say?) Joseph. Anyway, my address remains the same, my pockets empty, my spirits high, and my heart forgiving.

The boy who ran in to collect this letter was in fact named Joseph, and because he was cramming for his constitutional history exam he couldn't stay long; but Joseph at Felix's never was able to resist dropping down onto the floor for a few minutes, like a palace puppy.

"What brought you to this work?" he demanded, after reading the letter.

"What will bring you to the study of law?" was Felix's response.

"Though the old man must never know, I have a vocation. Keep it under your hat."

Felix, who happened to be wearing a burnoose, nodded.

"Do you have a vocation too?" asked Joseph. Without waiting for an answer, he said, "Your trade may land you in jail. As an accessory. Wilde's letter to Bosie helped convict him of moral obliquity. Dispatches hidden in a pumpkin convicted Hiss of treason. Dreyfus was found guilty because of a letter, the bordereau."

"And exonerated because of another letter, the *petit bleu*," said Felix in his easy way. "Hiss was convicted only of perjury, Joseph. I wish Wilde had been my client."

"You would have helped him with his problem?"

"Yes. His epistolary problem."

"Which was . . ."

"Excess," Felix confided.

Felix had never endorsed the theory that speech was what lifted man above other animals. To him, conversation was overrated and subject to abuse. "Let's talk things over, let's have an exchange," a husband would say earnestly to a wife, a teacher to a student, a world leader to another world leader, and the next thing you knew, out of the invisible untouchable space between two mouths there came a divorce, and a grade of F, and a war.

But letters could be touched and seen, could be hidden under a blotter, passed around at a funeral; could be crumpled, incinerated, or swallowed. Like certain animals and fairy princes, letters might undergo transformations. Like sauces, they could in the making be reduced first to perfection and then out of existence. Like diamonds and ballet performances and handmade sweaters, they were gifts. And if some people had difficulty parting with the gifts that were theirs to give, if some individuals needed help in this endeavor—why, that was fortunate for Felix and not so unfortunate for them. Their deficiencies were no disgrace. Were two left feet a sin? Or the inability to crochet?

Convinced of his calling, Felix had nonetheless been surprised by the success of his practice. He had been in business for five years and now had more requests than he could handle. His clients had included dissatisfied utility company customers and timid clerks and inhibited parents of first-time campers. He had worked on letters for the dying and disinheriting, for wastrels and prodigals. He had helped enlighten public officials, including the president. Felix had been summoned to chronic hospitals and to prisons. Certain letters he refused to have a hand in: anonymous ones, threatening ones, and obscene ones. He turned down pleas to write suicide notes. He would not do business over the telephone (he had no telephone). He sent out his bills monthly, he did not accept MasterCard (although if business ever dropped off he'd be glad to reconsider that policy).

His first afternoon appointment was with Miss Hanya. Miss Hanya wore her abundant gray hair in a bun. She was sending letters to a Mr. Mortimer, whom she had met last summer in Scotland. Felix charged her very little. For one thing, Miss Hanya's salary (she played the piano in a tearoom) was low. For another, Felix was sure that Mr. Mortimer did not exist—or, rather, that Mr. Mortimer was not an aged gentleman living quietly in a residential hotel in Edinburgh, but a bird, probably the black-whiskered vireo, whom Miss Hanya had met, exactly as she claimed, in a cobblestoned courtyard, and who had joined her for tea every day during her visit.

Miss Hanya had plump cheeks and wonderful skin, though she was not in her first youth. The romantic sweetness of her nature had to be allowed to reveal itself but not to romp all over the page. Felix employed judicious quotes from well-known poetry. He kept adjectives under strict supervision. He encouraged Miss Hanya to tell him about her day-to-day life, and as a result both he and Mr. Mortimer had learned a lot about the finances and clientele of the tearoom.

With Mr. Tratti, the next client, the challenge was to release the fellow's sentimentality while keeping the lid on his rage. Mr. Tratti had been a construction worker and now he owned a company. He had a wife and four children and one grandchild and a mistress and an ex-mistress. His mother still lived in a little brick house in Brooklyn with his sister Marcella, and she was kept alive, according to her own testimony, by his and Felix's communications. The weekly letters were better than any pacemaker, she said.

"The bitch," said Mr. Tratti that afternoon, squeezing himself into the customer's chair. "My sister Marcella the bitch is trying to talk Mama into selling the house. Move into an apartment, says Marcella. Neighborhood going downhill, she says. Stairs too many. Old lady too demanding. What Marcella really wants is to put the old lady away."

"Murder?" Felix inquired.

"Hey!" said Mr. Tratti, sensing an ethnic slur. "Nursing home."

"There are some good facilities. You could still write to your mother."

"Yes," said the fat man, leaning forward and spreading his hands on his knees. "And what will happen to a letter? Instead of going into the slot and dropping onto the sun porch floor—ah, that warm tile—and being picked up by Marcella, and being carried up to Mama on her lunch tray, and being opened by Mama, who says, Oh, from Vince, offhand, like she don't care; my eyes are too bad, says Mama; read it, Cella. Instead of that, what'll happen? Some nurse's aide will carry it around in her pocket for days. When she finally reads it to Mama, through her nose, she will skip whole paragraphs. Our letters, Felix, aren't meant for a *facility*. They're meant for 1160 East 23rd Street. I remember when we bought that house. Fifty-five years ago this week."

Felix took out a clipboard from his drawer. "Please tell me about the sun porch."

An hour later he was busy incorporating the sun porch into a letter of reminiscence, a short-sentenced letter in which the second person predominated. It would bring tears to Mrs. Tratti's eyes and to the bitch Marcella's, too. In the middle of yet another draft of that effort he was visited by Mrs. Wing, whose letters to the editor required Felix's assistance. Activists on behalf of children's television, said Mrs. Wing without preliminaries, were well meaning, but their heads were up their asses. It would be better to show nothing even halfway educational on the tube during the daytime, only shit. Then sensible parents would take a hatchet to the screen, and children would grow up without that glassy, goosed look. "That's the message," said Mrs. Wing, stuffing bits of paper back into her handbag. "Clean it up a little." At the door she turned and said, "Next to nuclear war, pesticides and contaminants are our greatest menace. Don't you think so?"

Felix adjusted his beret. "I don't think much about any of those things," he said courteously.

He finished Mr. Tratti's letter and wrote an outline of Mrs. Wing's, softening the righteousness as he cleaned up the scatology.

Now came a special time for the letter writer. Although it was almost evening, he hung out a cardboard that read Out to Lunch. Then he went into the back room and sat down crosslegged on the floor. With his clipboard on his knee, and nothing at all on his head, he began to write.

Dear Jennie,

I am glad that you found welcome the ten dollars I sent for your birthday. I wish that our organization allowed adoptive parents to send presents and not just money. Then you would have received also a new box of pastel crayons. Your drawings are beautiful. Lisa and I have put them on the living room wall. We especially admire the self-portrait in which your hand almost (but not quite) covers your smile. I noticed that the little bird flying off to the left is carrying a basket of missing teeth. He will bring back some new teeth when you are seven, Jennie. The wonderful picture of your mother and the new baby, with the foreshortened figure of your father floating next to your mother's ear, occupies a place of honor over our couch.

Will you send me another picture, even though I cannot send you crayons? Would you draw my little shop? The whole front of it is a door and a big window with many panes. The other three walls are white, and there is a gray rug on the floor. My desk is against one wall. There is a chair for me and also one for the client. That is all I will tell you, for that is all there is to see—all to see, though not all to suppose, especially when the supposer is the young lady who rendered two water buffalo playing chess, and called the work My Nice Uncles.

With fondest regards to you and your family.

Felix signed his name. Then, whistling, he stood up and went into the front room and folded the letter and put it and a check into an envelope and sealed the whole thing up.

For letters were a gift, and not to give the gift himself would have diminished Felix in his own eyes. It pained him to submit the letter to translation. He hoped that the translator was a monk with amnesia. Or maybe the organization engaged a series of lesser nobles, each of whom, after turning Felix's undistinguished handwriting into beautiful ideographs, fell onto his own sword. Whatever happened to the translators, Felix's letters belonged only to Jennie, and Jennie's only to him.

He went to the many-paned window. Night had fallen. Across the street the shops were lit up, and people were turning on lamps in upstairs apartments. Lisa would arrive soon. He looked forward to dining out with her and hearing about her busy, combative day. He fingered a white tie and adjusted his tails and performed a glide and a dip. Then he sat down at his desk to catch forty winks.

He didn't fall asleep right away. Instead, there unrolled on a platen in his mind Lisa's sobering forecast: that some day man might become embarrassed by hard copies of his sentiments. Bundles of letters would seem as odious as offal. Felix's trade would become obsolete. But the future wouldn't stop there. After a while, some scholar short of funds would notice that the skill of writing letters was being neglected. The nation might be at risk. Small grant would follow. Big grant next. Revision of high school curricula, founding of Epistolary Centers, formation of new college departments. Finally in the university itself would arise a school of correspondence, fighting dentistry and architecture for its portion of the annual gift. Felix, recalled from obscurity, would be given an honorary degree and an honorary chair; he would become an elder statesman, exalted and unheeded, salaried and unemployed.

Presently Lisa found him, snoring into his own elbow. The streetlamp shining through the shop window whitened his fair hair, giving him the look of a young man prematurely old or an old one preternaturally young. Who was that Greek who could change shapes at will?—Proteus. Proteus: a fellow very hard to pin down.

Felix raised his head. "When every man becomes his own inditer," he continued, "I'll turn to secrets. Stash your secrets with Felix, my card will read. I'll be a repository."

"Whatever you do, I'll mind my own business," Lisa said hopefully.

But he was already gone from her, dreamily imagining this secondary use of his discretion, his memory, his tolerance, and his good manners. Heads of state would come to him, financiers, ordinary bedeviled people. Psychiatrists. He could occupy these same premises. No flinging of hats at pegs, though; on entering the shop he would slowly unwind from his neck a long, inscrutable muffler, fitting accessory for a keeper of confidences.

INBOUND

~~~~~~~~~~~~~~~~~~~~~~~~~~~~~~~~~~~

On the subway Sophie recited the list of stations like a poem. Then she read the names from the bottom up. Saying something backwards made it easy to remember, sealed it in.

When the family got off at the Harvard Square station she frowned at a platform sign. "Outbound?" she asked her mother.

Joanna was bending over Lily's stroller, adjusting the child's harness. So Ken answered. "Outbound in this case means away from the center of the city," he said. "There are two sets of tracks, coextensive." He paused. Coextensive? Sophie had learned to read at three; her vocabulary at seven was prodigious; still . . . "They coextend," he tried. "One set of tracks carries trains outbound and the other carries them . . . ?"

"Inbound," said Sophie. "Then when we go back to the hotel we'll go inbound. But why aren't the inbound tracks next to these ones? Yesterday, under the Aquarium . . ."

Ken inhaled deeply; for a moment Sophie regretted getting him started. "This Harvard Square station used to be the terminus, the last stop," he told her. "When the engineers enlarged the system they ran up against the sewers, so they had to separate inbound and outbound

165

vertically." He had invented this explanation, or maybe he'd heard it somewhere. "Inbound is one level below us." That much he was sure of.

The family walked down a shallow ramp to the concourse. Sophie led the way. Her straight blond hair half-covered the multicolored hump of her new backpack, a birthday gift from her parents. During their early-married travels Ken and Joanna had worn explorers' rucksacks to out-of-the-way places. After Sophie was born they traveled only to France, always with their little girl. This venture across half the country was the first family excursion since Lily's birth two years ago. "An excursion is a loop," Joanna lightly explained to Sophie. "We start from home, we end up at home."

Ken, pushing the heavy stroller and its calm passenger, kept pace with Sophie. Joanna was at his heels, swinging the diaper bag and her scuffed brown pocketbook.

On the concourse Sophie paused. "The stairs are at the left," said Ken. Sophie started toward them, her parents like friendly bears behind her. Other people on the way out pushed through unresisting turnstiles, but because of the large stroller Ken and Joanna and Sophie and Lily had to use the gate near the token-vendor's booth. The stairway to the street was broad enough to climb together. Ken and Joanna lifted the stroller between them. All four, blinking, reached the white light of Harvard Square at the same time. Lily, startled and amused by the hawkers, made her familiar gurgle.

"Mama," she said to Ken.

"Dada, darling."

"Dada."

"Sophie, Sophie, Sophie," said Sophie, dancing in front of the stroller.

"Mama." She was not yet able to say her sister's name, though sometimes, on the living room floor, when Sophie was helping her pick up a toy, Lily would raise her odd eyes and gaze at the older girl with brief interest.

She had Down's syndrome. At two she was small, fair, and unfretful, though Ken and Joanna knew—there was little about Down's that they did not now know—that the condition was no guarantee of placidity. Lily was just beginning to crawl, and her muscle tone was improving; the doctor was pleased. In the padded stroller she could sit more or less erect.

"Lily clarifies life," Sophie had heard her father say to one of his friends. Sophie didn't agree. Clarity you could get by putting on glasses; or you could skim foam off warm butter—her mother had shown her how—leaving a thin yellow liquid that couldn't even hold crackers together. Lily didn't clarify; she softened things and made them sticky. Sophie and each parent had been separate individuals before Lily came. Now all four melted together like gumdrops left on a windowsill.

Even today, walking through the gates of the university that looked like the college where her parents taught, but redder, older, heavier; leaving behind shoppers in Harvard Square; feeling a thudding below their feet as another subway hurtled outbound or inbound; selecting one path within a web of walks in a yard surrounded by buildings . . . even today, in this uncrowded campus, they moved as a cluster.

"Massachusetts Hall," Ken pointed out. "The oldest building in the university. That's the statue of John Harvard over there. And dormitories new since our time—would you like to live here some day, Sophie?"

"I don't know."

Clumped around the stroller they entered another quadrangle. There was a church on one side and, on the opposite side, a stone staircase as wide as three buildings. The stairs rose toward a colonnade.

"That's the fifth biggest library in the world," her father told her.

"What's the . . . sixth?"

He smiled. "The Bibliothèque National in Paris. You were there."

Paris? Sophie recalled stained glass. They'd had to climb narrow, winding stairs to reach a second floor. Her mother, soon to give birth, had breathed hard. Blue light from the windows poured upon them— upon her tall, thin father, her tall, bulging mother, her invisible sister, herself. She recalled the Metro, too, as smelly as day camp.

"The Bibliothèque?" her father said again. "Remember?"

"No."

"Ken," said Joanna.

They drifted toward the fifth-biggest library. Joanna and Ken carried the stroller up the stone stairs. Sophie, in a spasm of impatience, ran to the top, ran down, flew up again. She hid behind a pillar. They didn't notice. She welcomed them at the entrance.

Inside, an old man sat at a desk inspecting backpacks. The family crossed a marble hallway and climbed marble stairs that ended in a nave of computer terminals. At last Lily began to whimper. They pushed the stroller into an area of card catalogs. Joanna picked Lily up. "We'll go into a big reading room," she crooned into the lobeless ear. "We'll look out a window."

Sophie watched them walk away—her mother so narrow in the familiar black coat. "Where are the books?" she asked her father.

"My little scholar," he said, and took her hand.

The entrance to the cave of books was just a door. An ordinary, freckled boy who looked like her high school cousin casually guarded the way. Her father fished in every pocket for the card that would admit them; finally he found it.

"Children . . ." began the boy.

"Ten minutes," promised Ken. Sophie had heard this tone reassuring a woman who had slipped on the ice in front of their house; he had used it also to soothe their cat when she was dying of cancer. "We're in town from Minnesota. I want her to see this treasure. *Five* minutes." The boy shrugged.

She followed her father through the door. Her heart, already low, dropped further, as when some playground kid shoved her. Upright books were jammed shoulder to shoulder within high metal cases, no room to breathe, book after book, shelf above shelf, case following case with only narrow aisles between. Too many books! Too many even if the print were large. This was Floor 4 East, said painted letters on the wall.

They walked up and down the aisles until they reached the end of 4 East. Then they turned; 4 East became 4 South. Behind a grille stood an aisle of little offices, all with their doors closed. She wondered what her mother was doing. Section 4 West came next. It was just like 4 East, books, books, books; a tiny elevator hunched among them. "Where does that go?" she whispered.

"Up to five and six," he whispered back. "Down to three and two and one and A and B . . ."

"Are the five minutes up?"

". . . and C and D."

This time it was Sophie who led the way—easier than she'd anticipated: you just hugged the perimeter. There was even an Exit sign. The freckled boy outside nodded at them.

Her mother waited next to the stroller. Lily was sitting in it again, sucking on a bottle.

Sophie kissed Lily seven times. "Was she impressed?" she heard her mother ask. "Awed," her father said. She gave Lily a ride, moving among card drawers on wooden legs.

Ken and Joanna watched their children appear and disappear.

"Those silent stacks," he said. "The elevator, where I first kissed you—I'd forgotten it." He kissed her again, lightly, on the elegant cheekbone that neither girl had inherited.

She kept her face raised, as if seeking sunlight. Then: "Let's try the museum," she said.

"Sophie will like the Renoirs," Ken agreed.

But at the museum Sophie found the *Seated Bather* spacey. Her father directed her gaze toward a painting of ballerinas haphazardly practicing. What was the point of that? Only one work caught her interest: substantial angels with dense overlapping feathers and bare feet reflected in the sand. "So you like Burne-Jones," he rumbled.

They were soon back on the street again, talking about lunch. Ken and Joanna decided on a favorite restaurant, hoping it still existed. They headed in its direction on a sidewalk next to the backs of buildings. "The library's rear door," Ken pointed. Sophie averted her gaze. They crossed the street at the traffic light.

That is, three of them did. Sophie, her head still awkwardly turned, got caught on the curb as the light flashed Don't Walk. Her parents lumbered away. Other people bore down upon her, blocking her view. By the time the crowd rushed past, the cars on the street had begun to roll again, and she was forced to stand still.

That was all right. Standing still was what she was supposed to do when she became separated from a parent. "If both of us run around, you see, the chances are that we'll never be in the same place at the same time," her mother had explained.

"Like atoms," said Sophie.

"I guess so . . . But if one of us stays put, the moving one will eventually cross the still one's path."

It made sense. Sophie had imagined that, in such an event, she would turn cool, a lizard under a leaf.

Instead she turned hot, even feverish. She sang "Go Tell Aunt

Rhody" under her breath, forwards. The sign changed to Walk. She sang "Rhody" backwards. Her mother would soon cross her path. But her mother could not leave the stroller. The sign changed to Don't Walk. Her father, then. He would stride across the street, two leaps would do it, he would scoop her up, he would put her on his shoulder, though she was much too big for such a perch; she would ride there for blocks and blocks; the restaurant would have a peaked roof and a lot of panes in the windows; they always chose restaurants like that.

Joanna had maneuvered the stroller rightward, had taken a step or two, had turned back for Sophie, had not seen her, had looked right, twice, and then left, down a pedestrian walkway, and had spotted amid a crowd of kids around a mime the fair hair and multicolored backpack of her daughter. Her heart bobbled like a balloon. "Where's Sophie?" said Ken at her shoulder. She pointed confidently and pushed the stroller close to the slanted window of a bakery. She'd lift Lily out and all three would have a good view of the mime—he was deftly climbing an invisible ladder—and of the delighted children, particularly Sophie in her new backpack and her old turquoise jacket, only that kid's jacket was green and she was taller than Sophie and her hair was yellower than Sophie's, much yellower, only an unnatural parent could mistake that common candle flame for her dear daughter's pale incandescence.

Sophie, telling herself to stand still, was jostled from behind. She turned to object, but the jostler had disappeared. The sign changed to Walk. Without forethought, though not unwillingly, she leaped into the street.

Sweaty, gasping, she fetched up on the opposite curb. She did not see her family. She saw strollers here and there, but none of them were Lily's; they were the fold-up kind for regular kids. She saw a wheel-chair. *That* wasn't relevant, she scolded herself, brushing her nose with the back of her hand. Lily would walk some day. A jester with a painted white face seemed to wave. She ignored him. She drifted toward the center of the square. Earlier she had noticed a newsstand . . . a kiosk, her father had said.

The newsstand turned out to be a bright little house of magazines and newspapers and maps. A man wearing earmuffs sat at a cash register. The place shook slightly every few minutes: the subway was underneath.

There Sophie waited, alone and unknown and free.

By now her parents would have retraced their steps. They had already crossed her empty path.

She felt most comfortable near the far wall. Foreign newspapers overlapped one another. There were French papers. She recognized *Le Monde* from that trip to Paris. *The World;* her father, if he were here, would request the translation. There were newspapers from other parts of Europe, too—she could tell that their words were Spanish or Italian, though she did not know the meanings. In some papers even the alphabets were mysterious. Letters curved like Aladdin's lamps, or had dots and dashes underneath them like a second code. Characters she had seen in Chinese restaurants stood straight up, little houses, each with a family of its own. Lily might learn to read, her mother had said. Not soon, but someday. Until that day, all pages would look like these, confusing her, making her feel more left out. Still, in a few years time she would be walking. She would stand close to Sophie. Maybe too close. What does it mean, she would whisper. What does it mean, she would whine, and pull at Sophie's sleeve.

The man with the earmuffs gave Sophie an inquisitive look. She turned to study a newspaper. Each word was many letters long, and each letter was a combination of thick and thin lines. She knew all at once that this was German. Her father played Bach on his harpsichord, from a facsimile of an old manuscript; the title and the directions were in German. If Sophie stayed in this pretty little house for the rest of her life she could probably learn one or two of the languages whose alphabet was familiar. Here was how she would do it: she would read the English papers thoroughly and then, knowing the news by heart, she would figure out the words' partners in the other papers. Maybe she'd start with Italian.

Joanna and Ken were behaving sensibly. Joanna was waiting near the mime, who was now walking an imaginary tightrope. He stopped, alarm on his painted face. He was pretending to lose his balance. His stiffened body canted slowly sideways in discrete jerks like a minute hand until at ten past the hour he collapsed into himself and in a wink became a man *hanging* from a tightrope, left arm upward and unnaturally long, right one waving desperately, legs splayed.

Ken had gone looking for Sophie. He would follow their route backwards to the museum, into the museum, from the Burne-Jones camp-counselor angels to the Degas and the Renoir. He would return to the library if necessary; Joanna imagined his tense interrogation of the man who inspected backpacks . . . The mime was collecting a thicker crowd; she had to crane her head to watch him. Sophie would enjoy this outdoor show once Ken found her, if she had not been snatched into a car, if she were not to end her life as a photograph on a milk carton. Joanna must not think that way, not not not; she must imagine normal outcomes like normal mothers, like mothers of normal children. The girl has wandered off, ruining our day because of some rush of curiosity, hyperintuitive they call her, *I* call her inconsiderate, doesn't she know enough to make things easier, not harder; don't we have it hard enough already with little Miss Misfit here, oh, my sweet Lily, my sweet Sophie, my darling daughters; and so I'll gaze at Lily dozing and think of Sophie when she was an infant and slept on her side in her crib with arms extended forward and legs too; she looked like a bison on a cave. I remember, I remember . . . *She* probably remembers, she with the genius IQ who can sing songs backwards. Ken loves to show off her memory and her queer talents, his prize onion. The mime's pedaling to safety; he's earned that applause. Haven't I got coins for his hat? But I can't leave the stroller, we can't leave each other, any of us. Of course Sophie will remember to stand still as soon as she realizes she's lost. Where would she go? She doesn't know this town. She's seen only the museum, she didn't like it, and the library, she hated it; Ken was hurt. She liked the subway. All kids like the underground: sewers, buried treasure, zombies. All kids like trains; they want to be headed somewhere, inbound, outbound . . .

Ken's face was putty.

"The library?" she needlessly asked.

"No," he panted.

"Come," said Joanna. "I know where she'll go."

Sophie, wriggling one arm out of the backpack, decided to start with the French newspapers. She was to study French next year anyway, with the rest of the special class. But she was pretty sure that she wouldn't soar with the new subject. She was tied to her first language, hers and Lily's. Still, she'd learn rules. She'd listen and sometimes talk. Now, staring at *Le Monde,* pretending that the man with earmuffs had gone home, she let her eyes cross slightly, the way she wasn't supposed to, and she melted into the spaces between the paragraphs until she entered a room beyond the newsprint, a paneled room lit by candles, walled in leather volumes, the way she had wanted the fifth biggest library to look. Though more books had been written than she could ever read—she had realized that as soon as she saw Section 4 East—she would manage to read a whole lot of them, in golden dens like the one she was seeing. She would read as many as her parents had read. She would grow as large as her parents had grown. Like them she would study and get married and laugh and drink wine and hug people.

Steadied by this vision, she let herself look further. Her life would be lived in the world, not in this paper house. She foresaw that. She foresaw also that as she became strong her parents would dare to weaken. They too might tug at her clothing, not meaning to annoy.

Lily would never leave her. "She will always be different, darling," her mother had said. At the time Sophie thought that her mother meant We will always be different. Now she added a new gloss: I will always be different.

Sophie felt her cheek tingle, as if it had been licked by the sad, dry tongue of a cat. At full growth Lily's head would be almost level with Sophie's shoulder. Lily would learn some things. Mostly she would learn Sophie. They would know each other forward and backward. They would run side by side like subway tracks, inbound and out-bound. Coextensive.

She had to return to her family now; she had to complete the excursion. She shoved her free arm into the strap and settled the back-pack on her shoulders. She walked past the man in earmuffs without saying good-bye.

Ken and Joanna bumped the stroller down the subway stairs. Ordinarily they would have joined the line at the token-vendor's booth to be admitted through his gate. Instead Joanna inserted a token and hurried through the turnstile. Ken handed her their little girl across the device. He pressed his own token into the slot and turned around and lifted the stroller above his head and burst through the stile buttocks first. They put Lily back into the stroller and rushed toward the ramps.

"Outbound?" said Ken.

"She knows better."

On the ramp they had to arc around an old woman who had paused midjourney with her trash bag on her left and her collapsible cart on her right. "That's okay," she called.

The inbound train had just left. The platform held five people who had missed it: three students, one bearded man, and a tall black woman—an Islander, Joanna could tell; her regality proclaimed her origins; I'll bet that magazine under her arm is in French.

Sophie wasn't far behind them. She had found the subway entrance as soon as she left the little house. While her father was bearing the empty stroller backwards through the turnstile, she was beginning her descent from the street. While her mother was choosing inbound, Sophie was thinking about joining the line of token buyers, of promising to pay later. She decided not to risk conversation with the man in the booth. By the time her parents reached the inbound platform she was slipping underneath the turnstile. She started down the ramp.

She saw them before she reached bottom. Her mother was sitting on a bench, holding Lily in her lap. Her father, standing, was bent over them both. They looked like everyday people, but Sophie wasn't fooled—her mother's knees were knocked together under her coat and her feet were far apart, their ankles bent inward so wearily that the anklebones were almost touching the floor. Without seeing her father's face she knew he was close to tears. An old woman with a cart was leaning against the wall. As Sophie appeared she said, "Now your reunion" in a conversational tone, though rather loud.

Ken turned and unbent: a basketball replay in slow motion.

Joanna took relief like an injection; pain was killed and feeling as well. She saw that the child had undergone some unsettling experience, but Joanna had no sympathy to offer now. Perhaps this once Sophie would be given the blessing of forgetfulness.

And indeed Sophie moved forward with a light tread, as if she had not just witnessed the future unscrolling.

Lily attended slackly. But then she raised her mittened hand.

"Phie!"

AFTERNOONS

～～～～～～～～～～～～～～～～

Maybe, as philosophers hint, we are all figures in another's dream. But perhaps instead we are the inventions of our associates, who helplessly concoct us as their stories demand.

One thing I'm pretty sure of: twenty years ago I spent a lot of time on benches.

At the tot-lot in the local park my young children easily made friends. I slouched against the slats and read, too solitary to join the groups of nannies, au pairs, Orthodox mothers wearing snoods, and in the summer, confident academics.

Alice turned up one July. Our children were the same ages—five-year-old girls and three-year-old boys. Alice too always carried a book. We began to occupy the same bench and to open our lunch sacks at the same time. I learned that her husband was a . . . manufacturer? Importer of leather? Something substantial. They had spent their first year of marriage in Latin America.

On a chilly September morning just before the beginning of school the kids played in moist sand and Alice and I shivered. It had rained all night. Before noon the rain began again. "Let's go to my house," Alice said.

We lived south of the park, on a close street of three-deckers. Alice lived on the north side, in a neighborhood of renovated Victorians. At a round kitchen table under a stuffed parrot—perhaps he was only cloth—we ate sandwiches and drank juice. Then the kids joyously commandeered a five-sided, glassed-in playroom separated from the living room by French doors, also glass. Alice and I settled with our novels on either side of the fireplace.

Outside the downpour continued. I felt a familiar ease. This phase of life was one long afternoon. At some distant time night would begin to flash and an orchestra would tune up. But for now, and for a while to come, the light was soft and the rain slipped silkily over the evergreens.

In the front hall the telephone rang. Alice crossed the room and disappeared. "Hello. Yes!" She talked for a few excited minutes. Then she returned to her chair and picked up her book without looking at me. The corners of her mouth were tight with pleasure and confusion.

After a while she remarked that her husband was on his way home; an old friend had come to town—a man they'd met in Chile. I think she said Chile, but it might have been Peru or Argentina. I think she told me he was a revolutionary and a physician, though perhaps she said doctor of philosophy. He was someone they once knew; I computed that much. Maybe she was too flustered to be altogether clear. Perhaps I was too lazy to be altogether attentive.

With a vague sense that we ought to be leaving I went into the playroom. The little boys had fallen asleep on mattresses. The little girls were busy with Legos. I sat down on a stool with my back to the living room and watched the sleeping children and the children at play and allowed my mind to slip again into the shallows of afternoon.

Behind my back, evening was beginning. A door slammed. Two deep voices sounded; above them Alice's alto soared; there were sentences in English and some in Spanish; I guessed an embrace.

I turned my head. A short man with a horseshoe of springy hair was beaming in the doorway. "Hi, Dad," said Alice's daughter, with the off-handedness of a loved child. My own daughter nodded in a perfunctory way. The little boys snoozed on. The balding man vanished.

The glass doors between playroom and living room were hung with netted curtains, certainly the work of some village cooperative. One door was closed. Alice's husband had left the other door ajar. I moved my stool so that I would be concealed, or at least blurred, by the door that was closed. I sat near enough to its curtain so that my eye could ignore the net squares and peer into the living room. I watched the couch. First it was empty. Then it was occupied.

The man was dark. He had the wide jaws and full lips of a bandit. He was enjoying a cigar. The upper part of his face had an intellectual cast—a high forehead, rich brown hair, wire eyeglasses. He took off the glasses. His suit was gray, and fine—the suit of a diplomat. Had Alice mentioned that he was now in his country's foreign service? Surely not; he had left Santiago after Allende's death; he had no truck with the present government; he was practicing international law, or international medicine, or international horse stealing. With those ripe lips and that overly reverent brow he was certainly not the handsomest man I had ever seen, but I couldn't think of anybody handsomer then, and I can't now.

Three adult voices in the living room lifted with laughter. The sound woke the little boys. They appeared at my knees, whimpering. I embraced them as if they were one child, or all children. I stood up and poured juice from the playroom pitcher.

"Maybe we should go home," I said softly to my son.

"No," he obliged.

The girls had abandoned their constructions and were playing checkers with chessmen.

"I'll read to you," I told the boys.

When, fifteen minutes later, the Chilean, without his cigar, came into the room, I was seated in an outsized wicker chair. My little son was wedged beside me. Alice's little son was astride my lap. I had managed to prop a book on my knee so that all three of us could look at the pictures while I read, and embellished, the minimal text.

I acknowledged the stranger's presence with a lift of the eyelids and a smile; but I was unhappily aware that my glasses had slipped halfway down my nose and that my hair was limp and not very clean.

He seated himself on the stool I had abandoned. The boys gave him the once-over and were apparently reassured by his quiet muscularity. The girls, now listening to the story, too, ignored him. I read until the end of the tale, and supplied my own cadenza. By popular request I read the last page a second time.

"You have a lovely voice," he said.

The five-sided glass room detached itself from the rest of the house. It whirled. I whirled within it. I was abruptly the heroine of my own life. The tranquil narrative I had been occupying for more than thirty years became, all at once, epic, tragedy, melodrama, and farce. I was ready to betray my husband and abandon my children. Alice would regret her hospitality.

"Oh," I managed to say.

The Chilean then got up and bowed and walked back into the living room. I dislodged the boys and staggered after him. All four children trailed *me*. In the living room—not glass, and not whirling—I collected myself somewhat. Dazedly I said good-bye. I received a handshake from each of the men—the Chilean's palm was rough—and a look of intense annoyance from Alice.

The rain had stopped. My children and I walked home through

the thick moist air, picking up cartons of Chinese food on our way—it was too late to think about cooking. My husband opened the door of the apartment before I could get my key out. "Where *were* you!" I saw that he had piled wood for a fire and had opened a bottle of wine.

I would like to relate two incidents:

(1) Last year, attending a symposium (I did eventually adopt a career), I became aware of a bulky man sitting in the front of the hall, three rows ahead of me and a little to the right. I could see his profile, and the set of his squarish head on his thick shoulders, and the glint of his glasses beneath his high brow. During the discussion period, he spoke twice. Each time he spoke he stood up, as if to make sure that everybody saw the long unseemly rip in his shapeless tweed jacket. His accent was pronounced. His comments were insistent and somewhat hostile, but the moderator parried them.

(2) In November I lingered in Jerusalem after my husband had gone home. On my last night I dined at a restaurant run by a correct Parisian. I sat at one of the best tables—as a woman alone I had attracted the Frenchman's cool protection. I gazed on the Old City, silver under the full moon. I was finishing my wine, and had fallen into a satisfied reverie, when a figure slid into the chair opposite. His cigar this time was slender.

"We met many years ago," he said. How sculpted his lips, how Argentine his hair. "You were telling a story to your children and to the children of some friends, and I have never forgotten the recess of your imagination, so rich, so urgent, which I was allowed for a few moments to enter."

As I say, I would like to tell these incidents, and even to embroider them freely. But neither is suitable to a reminiscence; for although both occurred, they occurred—to borrow the phrase—in the recess of my imagination.

So the Chilean must remain a figure of the distant, not recent, past. And perhaps he does not even belong there. We didn't see the other family again—the girls attended kindergartens in different schools, the boys different nurseries, and I couldn't telephone Alice, not after that parting glare.

My now grown children admit to no recollection of a five-sided, glassed-in playroom lashed by a September rain. As for the South American visitor, whom I sometimes mention, they affably dismiss him as another of those phantasms that Mom so frequently entertains; never considering that I may have been *his* phantasm, and Alice's, necessary to their story whatever it was.

PREVIOUS WINNERS OF
THE DRUE HEINZ LITERATURE PRIZE

The Death of Descartes, David Bosworth, 1981

Dancing for Men, Robley Wilson, 1982

Private Parties, Jonathan Penner, 1983

The Luckiest Man in the World, Randall Silvis, 1984

The Man Who Loved Levittown, W. D. Wetherell, 1985

Under the Wheat, Rick DeMarinis, 1986

In the Music Library, Ellen Hunnicutt, 1987

Moustapha's Eclipse, Reginald McKnight, 1988

Cartographies, Maya Sonenberg, 1989

Limbo River, Rick Hillis, 1990

Have You Seen Me?, Elizabeth Graver, 1991

Director of the World and Other Stories, Jane McCafferty, 1992

In the Walled City, Stewart O'Nan, 1993

Departures, Jennifer C Cornell, 1994

Dangerous Men, Geoffrey Becker, 1995

Grateful acknowledgment is made to the following publications in which some of these stories first appeared: *Alaska Quarterly Review* ("The Cook," "The Noncombatant," and "To Reach This Season"); *Ascent* ("Charity," "Donna's Heart," and "Rehearsals"); *Boston Globe Magazine* ("Inbound"); *Commentary* ("Settlers"); *New England Review* ("Felix's Business"); and *Witness* ("Cavalier" and "Dorothea").

Thanks also to Mishkenot Sha'ananim, in Jerusalem, where "Stranger in the House" was written.

This book was typeset in Stone Serif with Lithos display.
It was printed by Thomson-Shore, Inc.,
on 60 lb. Glatfelter Supple Opaque Recycled.

Library of Congress Cataloging-in-Publication Data

Pearlman, Edith, 1936–
Vaquita and other stories / Edith Pearlman.
p.   cm.
"The Drue Heinz Literature Prize."
ISBN 0-8229-3962-2 (cloth : acid-free paper)
1. Manners and customs—Fiction.   I. Title.
PS3566.E2187V37   1996
813'.54—dc20   96-10112